7 00

Moriah's Pond

Ethel Footman Smothers

Eerdmans Books for Young Readers
Grand Rapids, Michigan • Cambridge, U.K.

Text © 1995 by Ethel Footman Smothers
Previously published by Alfred A. Knopf, Inc.
This edition published in 2003 by Eerdmans Books for Young Readers
An imprint of Wm. B. Eerdmans Publishing Company
255 Jefferson S.E., Grand Rapids, Michigan 49503
P.O. Box 163, Cambridge CB3 9PU U.K.

03 04 05 06 07 08 09 10   8 7 6 5 4 3 2 1

Library of Congress Cataloging-in-Publication Data

Smothers, Ethel Footman.
Moriah's Pond / written by Ethel Footman Smothers.
p. cm.
Sequel to: Down in the Piney Woods.
Summary: While she and her older sisters are staying with their great-grandmother,
ten-year-old Annie Rye learns about prejudice firsthand when a local white girl causes
Annie's sister to be unjustly punished.
ISBN 0-8028-5249-1 (hardcover : alk. paper)
[1. Sisters—Fiction. 2. Great—grandmothers—Fiction. 3. African Americans—Fiction.
4. Georgia—Race relations—Fiction.] I. Title.
PZ7.S66475 Mo 2003
[Fic]—dc21
2002010134

Cover illustration by Ron Himler
Book design by Matthew Van Zomeren

To Delsey, Dana, and Dion, my wonderful daughters
who I hope will always remain sisters of the heart.

Author's Note

My great-grandma from my mama's side of the family was Moriah Peoples. But we mostly called her Myma. I can remember climbing on top of a whole stack of mattresses in her big old iron bed and falling asleep in the softness. Her house was a special place where I felt warm and safe.

Some of these memories from my childhood can be recalled as if they happened yesterday. Others have slipped away or never stuck in my mind. To bring them back, I rely on the recollections of my kinfolk, especially my sister, Laura (Brat) Williams, and my cousin, Charlie Mae Footman Hopkins. *Moriah's Pond* is based in part on incidents that took place in Camilla, Georgia, during the 1950s.

Contents

1. Free Information 1
2. Ash Cats 18
3. Washday 34
4. Dead Wrong 43
5. Moriah's Pond 49
6. Cupboards Store 57
7. Sore Eye 64
8. Wait And See .76
9. The Grudge 84

Chapter 1

Free Information

"Pssst . . . Annie Rye . . . Annie Rye. . ."

A crazy person over there whispering at me. And I knows it ain't nobody but Maybaby. So I just keep my eyes where I got'em at. On my fishing pole, "Maybaby, I ain't asking Moriah nothing" I says. But she keeps right on aggravating me. Won't even let me catch me no fish. She the most git-on-my-nerve sister I ever seen in my whole life.

"What, girl?" I frowns at'er.

"Go on, Annie Rye. Ask'er."

"I ain't gonna be moving from my spot. Not till I catches me a fish."

"You been setting in that same spot for I don't know how long and you ain't caught one yet." Maybaby got her mouth running, dabbing her pole in the water. "Anyway, them fish ain't going noplace," she reminds me. "They gon' be right here in this pond."

"I know they gon' be right here in this pond. You know why?" I tells'er. " 'Cause you keep stirring up the water. Keep yo' pole still, girl."

"But why you can't just do this one thing for me. Huh? Why you just can't go over yonder and ask Moriah if we can go in the pond?"

I sees Moriah halfway round the pond. Setting on a stepping stool. Minding her fish pole. She our great-grandma. But we don't call her that. We just say Moriah.

"I was thinking the same thing, Annie Rye. Why you won't go ask'er?" Now my other sister Brat pestering me. She squatting betwixt me and Maybaby, her fishing pole sticking straight up in the air. Brat or Maybaby neither one ain't got they mind on fishing. Both of'em older than me. But I'm smart for ten. Yes sir.

So I says to'em, "If y'all wanna go in the pond so bad, why don'tcha ask for your ownself?"

Maybaby hang her head down. She don't say nothing. But I knows why. 'Cause they scared Moriah gon' tell'em go straight to the house and scale them fish. So Maybaby she still trying to push me up to do the asking. You wouldn't think she was old as she is. Going on fourteen. Two years more than Brat. And over there whining just like a baby. Listen at'er.

"You might as well go on. If you don't, you know how it gonna be when we git back to the house."

I knowed all right. Sweaty hot. Setting on the front porch shelling peas and fanning gnats. So I says to'em, "This one time I'm gon' do this 'cause I wanna be nice to ya." I pulls my pole out the water and lays it on the ground. "Ain't gon' git no fishing done no way. Witcha scaring'em and going on. "

I ease over to Moriah. Talking down to her ear.

Moriah." I says real soft.

"Huh," she says back to me. Still watching her cork stopper.

"Moriah," I whispers again. This time she take her eye off what she doing.

"Li'l Rye." Now she looking in my face. Like she ain't had no notion it was me. Li'l Rye what she call me 'cause I be named after her. Annie Moriah.

"Child, where yo' pole at?"

"Down there." I point back where Maybaby and Brat eyeing me. "Ain't been catching none," I tells'er. Looking all pitful.

"You ain't?"

"No'm."

"Well now, we can't be having that." She pat the backa my leg and I look pitful as I can.

"No'm. And I knows why I ain't caught none. This morning when Brat saw the hem of my dress turned up. You remember? 'Fore we come down to the pond?"

Moriah nod her head. So I go on telling her what done happened.

"She kiss her finger and touched the flipped-up part and says, 'I got your luck.' And I ain't had a specka luck since."

"Now. Now. There ways of fixing that. Run along bring Granny yo' pole." She pat my leg again and smile in my eye.

"Didja ask'er yet?" Maybaby and Brat ask one after the other, when I make it back where my pole at.

"Nope," I tells'em. "Gotta catch me a fish."

I grab my pole and take back off where Moriah at. She mush up stuff outa tin can and spread some on my bait. And before my line hit the water good I feels jerking on my pole. When I snatch it up, a big ole fish just flicking every which way. Ooou-we-e-e! Moriah really know how to make them there fish come to your pole all right. She sho nuff do.

Moriah smile one of her "m-m-m-huh" smiles. Like when she knows what she knows. Then she push down on her knees and stand up.

"These bones ain't what they used to be, Li'l Rye. Stiffening up on me. Old age setting in."

"You ain't old," I tells her. "Uncle Curry say don't nothing git old but clothes."

Moriah laugh.

"Well, let me git on back to the house," she says, uncrumpling her apron. "I wanna run a few of these fish by Maylene's. And I want y'all to come on directly."

"Moriah," I says when she fixing to take her pole, "I was wondering if we, Maybaby and us . . ." I point down where my sisters at and back at me. "If all us could go in the pond?" I don't give Moriah a chance to answer back. I just go on talking. "I knows I gotta help you shell peas and Maybaby and them gotta clean fish." I looks down at the ground and back up at Moriah. "But we just wanna take a little dip."

Moriah pick up her fish bucket. "If y'all can manage to be back at the house before long, I don't see where it gon' hurt nothing."

"We will, Moriah," I says as she going up the trail.

"See to it now," she call back.

"We will," I says again. Then I signal for Maybaby and Brat. And they come running.

First thing Maybaby wanna know, "What she say?"

I push between'em. "She say last one in a stink bug."

"Well I ain't gon' be one!" Maybaby stripping down to her underskirt. Same as me.

"Well I sho ain't gon' be one!" Brat racing to the pond 'long wit me and Maybaby. Her dress halfway off. We flop in at the same time. Sending water every which way. Laughing and dunking and going on.

Then all us wade out to the deep part where the old oak tree got a limb dipping down in the water like a crooked elbow. I hoist myself up on the level end. Maybaby and Brat hoist up too. And all us lay 'cross the big ole branch, faces looking in the water.

"Y'all . . ." I says from my spot in betwixt'em. "Y'all, what'll happen if I falls on my head in this here water?"

Maybaby raise up a bit. "You'll be wetter than you is."

We all laugh out loud. Hunching one another and going on.

"This the bestest, Annie Rye. Ain't it?"

"Uh-huh," I says, bobbing my head at Brat's reflection. Upside-down plaits sticking up behind her ear like cow horns. Yep, this was the bestest all right. The bestest ever.

Me and Brat and Maybaby here at Moriah's 'cause Mama and them don't be needing us in the field just yet. Elouise—she the baby—and Brother, they back in the Piney Woods with Mama and them. Doris—she my big sister—she staying over at Hun's, over on Route 3. Hun, she Moriah's sister, our auntie. But we don't call her that. We just say Hun. Just like we call Moriah, Moriah. And this pond be Moriah's Pond.

I been doing me some thinking 'bout this pond and all. Since this pond got Moriah's name and I'm named after Moriah and got her name, seems to me this pond named after me. Same as her. But I don't be bragging on it or nothing. Moriah say it don't look good. Bragging. Bringing up stuff in people's face. Thinking you more than you is. So I don't say nothing. Not one mumbling word. But I be knowing ain't no colored folks hereabouts got them no pond named after them. Not in all Mitchell County, Georgia. No sir. Just me and Moriah.

My mind way off someplace else. Dreaming in space, Moriah calls it. So I don't even notice somebody nudging me. Till Brat she do it again.

"Annie Rye . . . look."

"Where?" I says, raising up.

"Over yonder."

I looks where Brat pointing at a whole slew of hogs running wild. Heading straight for the pond.

"Who's that running behind'em ?" Maybaby say.

"Mr. Homer," I tells'er. I knowed it was Mr. Homer

when I see his spider arms waving in the air. Trying to head them hogs off. But them hogs got a mind of they own. And they wind up in the pond anyhow. Pretty soon Mr. Homer he in the pond too. Next thing, we don't see no Mr. Homer. All we sees is one spider arm sticking up amongst them hogs. And we all bust out. Just laughing.

Soon as we inch down to the ground, we gather up our clothes and sneak behind some bushes. Giggling and going on, while we stepping out our wet underskirts and slipping our clothes back on. All the way back to the house we laughing and talking about Mr. Homer and them hogs.

Moriah setting on the front porch shelling peas. Uncle Curry, he there too. All reared back in his straight chair. Leaning against the house.

"You oughta seen Mr. Homer," I says to'em. "Him amongst all them hogs."

"Heard'em all the way up to the house." Moriah look off towards the pond. Still shelling peas. "It's a wonder Mr. Daniels' hogs didn't run right off in the pond."

Uncle Curry fanning hisself. "Couldn't blamed'em if they had. Dog bite'it."

Us three bust out laughing again.

"They did," Maybaby says, trying to catch her breath, "and took Mr. Homer 'long wit' em."

We bust out again. 'Bout to split a gut. Moriah do too.

"Musta been a sight to see," she says, trying to put on a straight face. "Well, seems like y'all done cooled off some too."

"We did," I says right quick.

"Then I think it's high time you got to yo' duties."

Maybaby and Brat head round to the back so's they can hang our underskirts on the line and start scaling Moriah's fish.

Then I grab me a lap full of peas. Glad I ain't round on the back. Now I can hear me some talk 'bout them olden days. "Moriah," I says, setting on the edge of the porch. "How long you been living on this place?"

Moriah takes her a deep breath. "Been here quite a spell. More years than I wanna count. Moved in shortly after yo' great-grandpa Greene passed on." Moriah chuckle to herself. "Some folk said Greene was a odd sorta name. Nothing was odd about my Greene. Naw sir." Moriah look up from her pea shelling. Gazing 'cross the road.

"I know all about him," I says, drawing Moriah's eyes down at me. I knowed all about Mr. Ralph Daniels, too. He the white man owns all the land down in these quarters. Owns the piece Moriah staying on too.

"And way 'fore you was born," she go on, sliding peas out the hull, "I owned my own land. Every stick on it. That was when yo' great-grandpa Greene was still up and walking around."

"And then after he was dead and gone, it went to some other folk. Didn't it, Moriah?" I knowed all about that, too. How them white folk took it. Stole it right from under Moriah's nose. "And that's how you come to be at Mr. Ralph Daniels' place. Ain't it, Moriah? And he the one named that pond after you. Didn't he, Moriah?"

Moriah smile. "You done heard it so often, child, you practically know it by heart."

"I know," I says, sticking my chest out. "Be knowing 'cause I be listening." I scoop a handful of peas I done shelled outa my lap and put'em in the dishpan. Uncle Curry he still got his chair leaning against the house. He favor Moriah some. Only thing, Moriah she short and stout, and wears a apron all the time. And Uncle Curry he tall and straight just like a sticka cane.

"Uncle Curry," I says, looking up at him. "Uncle Curry, did you like being a railroad man? Laying down all them tracks?"

"All 'em tracks." Uncle Curry says after me. He just about always do that. Say the last words you do before he go on.

"Sot down a many of 'em in my day. Musta been a skillion or mo'," Uncle Curry says all slow like. 'Cause that's how he talk. All slow like. Dragging out his words. One after the other. "Sot down so many of 'em. Could see'em in my sleep. Stretching from hither to yon. Miles and miles of 'em."

"And then you used to be a traveling man. Riding on them choo-choo trains. Didn't you, Uncle Curry?" I look over at him and he open his mouth like he fixing to say something. But I don't wait to find out. I just keep right on talking.

"And all you had to do was run alongside that train and hop on real quick. Shoot, Uncle Curry, hitch yourself a ride just like that. All for free. Didn't hafta pay one red cent."

I pile my hulls in a heap. "'Yep. Uncle Curry, you sho knowed how to make yo'self a real good living. Going where you please. When you please. And I heard you was a fine young rooster back in them days. Just struttin' yo' stuff."

"Struttin' my stuff. Hah!" The corners of Uncle Curry's mouth inch up to a wide grin. Then he laugh out real loud. "You know it. Dog bite'it."

Uncle Curry slap his knee. And I slap mine. "Dog bite'it." I laugh out loud, and Uncle Curry he laugh again too. He like talking about what went on in them olden days. Not everything though. So I don't mention nothing about it. How this one time something happened on one of them trains and Uncle Curry come home on a walking stick. Been here ever since. Staying right here with his sister Moriah. Uncle Curry he old now. Almost old as Moriah is. And won't let nobody do nothing for him. Says he been seeing after hisself all these many years, he can keep on doing the same.

One time he was shooting out the window with his shotgun, aiming at one of them guineas and his gun kicked back and Uncle Curry hit the floor. Wham. And I says to him, "Uncle Curry, you hurt." And he tells me, "Hush up, gal. Go on 'bout yo' business." So I do. I leaves him alone and go on about my business. Let him pick his ownself up off the floor.

Uncle Curry was peculiar that way. Not wanting

nobody fussing over him or nothing. He was peculiar about his clothes, too. Won't wear colored shirts neither. Just white ones. Wore 'em all the time 'long with his suspenders. Don't know why. He just do.

I put all the peas in the dishpan and then Moriah tells me to go see how Maybaby and them coming 'long scaling them fish. 'Cause she got to git her pots to boiling. So I make haste and go on round back where Brat and Maybaby cleaning them fish at. 'Longside the house, on the wash bench where Moriah got her tin tubs hanging.

"Y'all almost done?" I says to'em.

"Nearly about." Maybaby grab another fish and rake scales off. Then I sees she done missed a spot. So I says, "Maybaby, you done left some scales on that one. Right yonder."

Maybaby look at me, rolling her eyes. She don't say nothing. Just roll her big ole eyeballs to the side. Then go on raking scales off with a teaspoon. I sees Maybaby just wanna be acting ugly. In one of her moods.

"I was just trying to give you some free information."

"Well I got news for you." Maybaby just jerking her head and going on. "We don't want none of your free information."

"All right," I says to her. "One day you gonna wish you had some and you ain't gon' be able to git none." I lets my head wobble from side to side. Just like Maybaby. "Know what I mean, jelly bean?"

"Annie Rye, didn't nobody ask you nothing. And just so you know. We don't need you overseeing nothing we doing." Maybaby cut her eyes at Brat. "Do we?"

Brat don't answer her back. She don't even take up for me. She just keep on pulling guts out. So I sticks my head in between'em. "Didn't hafta. I was giving you some just the same." I catch hold of Maybaby's plait and yanks it real hard. Maybaby draws back her arm and I jump back so's she can't reach me.

"Miss-aah-sippi," I says, poking fun at'er.

"Annie Rye girl, you better quit. What's ailing you?"

"Nothing ain't ailing me."

"Then why you cutting up?" Maybaby wants to know. "Why you being so fast and acting womanish?"

"That's for me to know and you to find out," I says, strutting back and forth.

"Aaahh Annie Rye, go on in the house." Maybaby shaking her head. "You pitful. Just plain pitful."

I turn around to say something back and before I do, Maybaby and Brat tells me at the same time, "Go on in the house." But I don't. I just set at the other end of the wash bench and look at Maybaby and Brat popping them scales every which way.

"Maybaby," I says to her, "you think that fish knows he a fish?"

"I know you ain't got no sense." Maybaby looks at me all disgusted. "You how old, Annie Rye?"

"Old a nuff to sleep in a bed without falling out." I grins at'er.

Now Maybaby rolling her eyes at me again.

"My goodness," I says, flinging my arms in the air and

12

bobbing my head to the side. "I just ask a simple question. That's all."

"Ain't nothing simple around here, Annie Rye, but you."

"Well," I says, looking her dead in the face, "I just figured you and Brat oughta know 'cause y'all older than me. But since ya don't, I guess that makes ya more simple than me. Don't it?"

"Aw hush, Annie Rye, and go on in the house," Maybaby tells me. So I do.

The house ain't parted off in small parts like a house s'pose to be. You can see straight through. From one end to the other. All except for Uncle Curry's room. He got him a little one all by hisself. And the rest of us sleep out in the open part. Up towards the fireplace.

Now I sees Moriah in the kitchen washing peas. So I go on the porch where Uncle Curry at and lean me a chair back just like him. Soon as I do, I sees a car coming. Bringing dust with it. The next thing I know, it done pulled right up out front. And I knowed who it was even before it stopped. Betty Jean and her mama.

I could tell 'cause Betty Jean was hanging out the window with a soda water. Betty Jean always had a soda water. Just like she do now. And before the car turned off good, she out coming up to the porch. Big ole bow ribbons plastered on her head. Then her mama git out too. Right behind her. Toting a basket of ironing. Betty Jean's mama was tall and lean. Not a ounce a fat on'er. And her hair was the same color as straw. Just like Betty Jean's.

I poke my head in the window and hollers for Moriah. "Moriah, Miz Riggs here."

Miz Riggs rest her elbow on the basket of ironing she done brought for Moriah and start talking to Uncle Curry. He still got his chair propped up. Leaning against the house. I sets my chair up straight flat on the floor. So's I can see what she gon' say. But I don't be looking down her throat while she talking 'cause Moriah say that's being ill-mannered. So I don't look straight in her mouth. I just look on the side. Where her jaw at.

"And how you gitting along, Uncle Curry?" she says to him, her jaws stretching and going back in place. She always call Uncle Curry uncle. But the plain truth is she ain't no kin to him a'tall. 'Specially him being colored and all. White folks just called some colored people that. Uncle and auntie. I ain't figured out why. They just do.

Uncle Curry he don't be mad or nothing. He just nod at'er and tells'er, "Gitting along. Faring right nicely," he says, putting in the last words she done spoke. "Yes'm. Faring right nicely."

"Well, you keep seeing after yourself. Now you hear?"

Uncle Curry he nod at'er again. Then I sees her watching the door.

Moriah come out toting one of her double-decker jelly cakes. More than three stacks high.

Miz Riggs push the ironing to one side. Her eyes fasten on that jelly cake Moriah done made. She always fix her one the first Monday in the month.

"Moriah, you outdone yourself this time. I declare,"

she says, reaching for the sweet bread that got apple jelly spread all on it. "Moriah, this got my mouth to dripping and I ain't even cut it yet."

"And don'tcha go cutting it neither, Miz Riggs," Moriah tells'er. "That cake for yo' tea party. And you need something to set it in so's you can take it home in one piece.

"Brat," Moriah hollers back in the house. "Bring me something to set Miz Riggs' cake in."

Brat come out the door swinging a dishpan. Moriah give her a hard look. So Brat just let it rest by her leg.

"This oughta do quite nicely," Moriah says, smiling down at Miz Riggs. Her and Betty Jean still standing on the ground. "My gracious. Look at me. Forgitting my manners. Make yo'self at home," Moriah says, offering her a seat.

Uncle Curry set his chair up straight. Flat on the floor. "C'mon up here. Take a load off yo' feet."

"Don't mind if I do," Miz Riggs says, taking the last straight chair.

Betty Jean she still standing in the same spot. Sipping on that soda water.

"Li'l Rye," Moriah says, looking at me. "Move and let Betty Jean have yo' seat. So's she won't git her dress dirty."

I cut my eyes down at the floor. Why I hafta give my seat to Betty Jean? She ain't no company. She ain't no bigger than me.

Now Brat hunching me in the side. "Annie Rye, you

heard."

I felt just like saying, "Sho I heard. I ain't deaf. I can hear." Shoot. What you think I got ears for? I says in my mind, inching out the chair so's Betty Jean can have my seat.

"She don't have to give me her chair," I hears Betty Jean say to Moriah. "I stand up all the time."

I look up at'er and Betty Jean she grinning over a empty soda water bottle.

I cut my eyes at Moriah and she gives me a nod. So I knows it must be all right for me to keep my seat. To set right where I'm at.

Then Betty Jean come around the porch. Standing with her arms pulled behind her back. Like she trying to think up something to say. She look down at the ground, then back up at me and Brat.

"Y'all been finding doodlebugs under this here porch?"

"Some," I says to'er.

"I don't git a chance to hunt doodlebugs much," she says, smoothing the front of that fancy dress she got on. Then she suck her breath in and let it out real slow like.

"Gramps he say it ain't ladylike." Betty Jean nod towards Mr. Ralph Daniels' place up the road, then go on and finish her words out. "Says I ain't got no business scrounging under the house like no common ordinary—" Betty Jean stop right in the middle of what she saying and look down at the ground. "But I'd like to go witcha sometime."

16

I don't say nothing. Just watch Betty Jean screw her patent leather shoe round in the dirt. Then I hears her say, "Got some licorice in the car. Y'all want some?"

Me and Brat's eyes meet. Mostly we don't know what to make of Betty Jean. She sho don't act like no white person I know. Not unless it was Miz Riggs. Betty Jean's mama. She strange too. I ain't figured neither one of'em out yet. 'Specially Betty Jean. The way she always up in me and Brat's face. Offering us stuff. Just like she doing now.

"Take one," she says, holding the paper sack out in front of us. And Brat don't waste no time. She grab her one right quick. I look down at the paper sack, then back at Betty Jean. I start not to take none. But Brat hunch me in the side.

"Go on, Annie Rye. Take one."

So I do.

"Betty Jean nice. Ain't she, Annie Rye?" Brat tells me after they gone.

I knowed Betty Jean wasn't like other white folks and all. That's for sho. But Uncle Curry say you gotta watch out for a dog always toting you a bone 'cause sooner or later he gon' turn on ya.

Chapter 2

Ash Cats

Early next morning Moriah up and gone to Mr. Ralph Daniels' house. She do housework for him and do the washing and ironing. And keep everything all straightened up. She do the cooking, too. So she don't fix nothing here at the house all the time. We just go up the road so's she can fix us something soon as she done fixing Mr. Ralph his. All us go—me, Brat, and Maybaby. Riding on Moriah's mule, Gertude. And we setting steady too. All except for Brat. She keep sliding off.

"I'm tired of slipping off the back end of this mule." Brat pick herself up off the ground. "I come out better just walking."

"Not me. I'm gon' ride," I says, scooching up behind Maybaby. "I'm gon' ride all the way where Moriah at."

"And when we git there, don't go putting your hands on nothing." Maybaby looks over her shoulder at me and I frown up at'er.

"Who said I was gonna go touching something?" I says to'er.

"Well, I'm just reminding you 'fore you do."

"You don't hafta go reminding me 'bout nothing, Maybaby. I'm not simple-minded like you." I slide off Gertude and walk in the back where Brat at. Who Maybaby think she is? Trying to tell me what to do. Trying to rule over me. She not grown, and I don't hafta be minding her. And she knows it too. But naw, Maybaby just gotta have her liver lips flapping. Shoot. I know what Moriah done said. Keep my hands to myself.

And that's just what I do when we come in the kitchen at Mr. Ralph Daniels'. Keep my hands to myself. Got'em right in my lap. And I don't take them out no more until Moriah placing our plates on the table. Filled with grits and brown gravy. And me and Brat don't waste no time sopping them plates clean. Then Moriah she come back and set'em in the dishpan.

"Ain't good gobbling yo' food down that way," she warns. "Next thing you know, you gon' wind up with a bellyache."

"They just hogging it down." Maybaby laugh. "Act like they ain't had no food in I don't know when."

I look off from the table. I ain't gon' be wasting my breath on Maybaby. I ain't listening at a word she saying. I ain't studying about you, Maybaby, I says to'er in my mind. Then I hunch Brat, and me and her go to slapping our hands up against one another's and saying our saying.

> *"God bless the table*
> *And God bless the cook*
> *All who ain't had a nuff—*
> *Stand up and look."*

19

Moriah she got her back turned doing something else. So I ease up from the table where I'm setting at and peep around the corner.

We all not allowed in no other part of the house. Except for Moriah. We just stay in the kitchen. We not s'pose to pitter-patter all over the big eating room neither. The one next to the kitchen. That's where Mr. Ralph got that big ole glass case. White folks calls it a china cabinet. Moriah she just call hers a safe. That's where she set her sweet bread after it done cooled. But Mr. Ralph don't. He keep ashes in his. Dead people ashes. Brat don't wanna sneak her a peep, 'cause she scared. Not me. Shoot no. I ain't scared of no ole ashes in no jar. Anyway, Uncle Curry say dead folks can't do you no harm. It's the live ones you gotta watch out for. So I ain't scared one bit.

Then I feels something tapping me on the shoulder. Standing right behind me. And I almost jump outa my skin.

"Maybaby! Girl, whatcha doing sneaking up on somebody like that," I hollers at'er. "Stop pecking on me."

"Moriah say come away from there. And stop being so nosy." Maybaby right in my face.

"Girl, git from under me. I can't even breathe." I push pass Maybaby and go out the back door. Brat she come too. We go down the steps, and sees Betty Jean. She setting on a tree swing way 'cross the back yard in one of them dress-up dresses. I ain't even knowed she was here. Now she beckoning for me and Brat to come where she at. Under the tree shade. But we don't go nary step. We just stand by the steps wit our hands behind our backs. Looking at'er. So Betty Jean she do it again. Motion for us.

"You going, Annie Rye?" Brat whisper in my ear.

I hunch my shoulders up. Knowing most likely I ain't. So Brat she nudge me.

"Why you don't wanna go over where she at?"

I wall my eyes up at the sky and pop my tongue. "Tck. Shoot, I ain't thinking 'bout that girl. She got feet. Why she can't come over here?"

"I don't know why you act that way towards Betty Jean. She never done nothing to us. She always try to be nice."

"M-m-m-huh. Yeah she always trying to be nice. But why she trying?"

Brat hunch her shoulders up. "Could be just 'cause she wanna. How ya gonna know if you don't give'er a chance? Maybe she ain't got no brothers or sisters or nothing. Maybe she ain't got nobody like we do." Brat lean over next to me, and I hug'er up. Smiling at'er.

"I'll go witcha this time. But I ain't trusting no Betty Jean," I says, following Brat.

"Hey y'all," Betty Jean says right off, swinging back and forth wit her feet flat on the ground. "Whatcha been doing? Where ya been?"

I feels just like saying:

> *"Been in my skin—*
> *When I jumps out*
> *You jump in."*

And Brat knows I fixing to say it too. So she poke me in the side. And I just let Betty Jean go on talking.

"There ain't no colored younguns round here. No chilluns hereabouts a'tall. Nobody but y'all." Now Betty Jean looking at the ground. "Told Gramps there ain't nothing to do. And he say I don't hafta do nothing. Just look pretty." Betty Jean eyes come up where mines at. "By jimmykins. That's about much fun as a plate of cold grits."

Brat she laugh. I don't. I just give a little halfway one, ain't hardly a grunt. Then I say to'er, "Well you sho can't be doing nothing in that fancy dress. It'll be messed up 'fore you know it. And you sho can't be doing yo'self no somersaults." I turns one right quick and lands straight up.

Betty Jean eyes grow all big. So I tell'er, "I can climb up a tree too. Just like that," I says, snapping my fingers.

"Ain't you scared people gon' see your bloomers?"

Now Betty Jean eyes real big.

"Naw. I ain't scared. 'Cause if they ain't seen none yet, when they do, they gon' see they ain't missing nothing."

Betty Jean laugh. Brat do too. But I don't let my dress hang loose. I tuck it between my legs, tied in a knot. Then right quick I hoist myself up on a limb and reach out for another one. I inch way out and hang upside down by my legs. Just like a ole possum.

"See what I tell ya?" I says, showing'em what I can do. "Even a bloodhound couldn't catch me 'fore I got up here."

"You fast all right," Betty Jean say. "I could never do that. All I do is swing in the swing. Y'all wanna swing some?"

I drop down out the tree and land in a squat. When I straighten up, Brat setting in Betty Jean's swing. Fixing to push off. "You know how to pump?" she ask Betty Jean.

Betty Jean shake her head.

"Nothing to it," Brat tells'er. "Easy as pie. Me and Annie Rye we pump all the time."

"Let's pump then." Betty Jean all glad, hopping in the swing the wrong way.

"You can't pump that way," Brat says to'er.

"Then let's just swing like this first," she says, standing up same as Brat. Now she telling me to start'em off. Give 'em a little push. At first I think I ought not. Then I sees Brat working her mouth. And I know what she saying. 'Cause I can read her lips. So I go ahead and gives them a good push and they go way high. Arms round each other. Side by side. Giggling and going on. And I just fixing to give'em another good pushing when I hear somebody holler.

"Betty! Git in here!"

I knowed who it was even before I turn around. Mr. Ralph Daniels. Betty Jean's granddaddy. He got that clogged-up sound in his voice. Like somebody done stuffed cotton all up his nose. He hollers again.

"Betty. You hear? Come in the house!"

I could tell Mr. Daniels didn't like Betty Jean being out here wit us. Didn't like it none a'tall. She and Brat being up in that swing like they was. Arms round one another. Betty Jean and Brat knowed it too. So right quick they come untangle and Brat she jump down. Then Betty Jean do the same. Just like Brat. Only she land belly down in the dirt. Shame all over her face.

Next thing we know, Betty Jean running to the window where Mr. Daniels at, pointing at me and Brat. Uh-oh. I know we in deep trouble. Betty Jean over there running her mouth. Telling on us. I know she gonna say it's our fault she done fell out that swing. I know I shoulda never trusted her.

Now Moriah gon' git us for sho. Brat knows it too. 'Cause she got a worried look on her face. Just like me. So we don't even say bye to Moriah or nothing. We just sneak where Gertude tied by the fence and wait for Maybaby.

And all while we on our way back to the house, I got my mind on what done happened. 'Cause I just bet for sho Betty Jean laid the blame on us. And not only that. Maybaby she acting stupid again. It ain't like I didn't say nothing. 'Cause I did. Three times in a row. Just got through saying it again. "Girl, I'm scorching." But Maybaby don't pay me no mind a'tall. She go on leading Gertude down this dirt road. And it stretching long and hot. Like we ain't never gonna make it back to the house.

"Don't know why we out in all this heat," I says, pushing my mouth way out. "Don't know why we hafta go traipsing off to Mr. Ralph Daniels' all the time like this neither. Could just eat what Uncle Curry done cooked."

"You know Moriah not gon' have that, " Maybaby says before I got my words out good.

"But why?" I frowns up.

" 'Cause she ain't."

"But Uncle Curry can cook good. I tasted some of his cooking before."

"Annie Rye, just walk up, girl. So's you can catch some of these bundles in case they start sliding off Gertude."

"But why we hafta do this all the time? I'm hot."

Maybaby turn around and prop her hand on her hip. " 'Cause we gotta take Mr. Ralph Daniels and 'em's ironing back to Moriah's so she can do it. And 'cause Moriah said so. Is that good a nuff for you?" Maybaby turn back around, blowing her breath out real hard. "So quit grumbling."

"I ain't grumbling. I just wanna ride."

"Well you can't. Gertude got enough to tote."

"That's what mules s'pose to do," I say. "Tote stuff. That's what they made for."

"And yo' feet made to walk on," say Maybaby. "So walk."

Ah dooley squat. There she go again. Maybaby trying to act like the big boss. But she ain't so much. So I tells her flat out, "I'm gon' stop under that shade and rest."

Maybaby whirls around. "No you ain't. You better try and walk up like Brat."

Brat steady stepping down the road. Wiping sweat. She not saying nothing. Just looking down at the ground.

But I ain't gon' hush. Not me. Shoot no. If I got something on my mind, I'm gon' say it. Yes sir.

"Maybaby, I feel like a parched-up 'tato."

"Annie Rye, you pitiful." Then she bust out laughing. "Girl, you a sorry sight. Now you done got your gut full you wanna crawl up somewhere and take a nap. Just like colored folks."

"Don't you go badmouthing colored folk," I hollers at'er. "You ain't white. You colored. Just like the resta us."

Maybaby don't say nothing back. She just look straight ahead. Holding on Gertude's rope. So I cocks my head to one side and start humming to myself. Thinking about how good it gon' feel to go wading in the pond and cool my feet off. "Wanna go wading when we git to the house?" I says to Brat. Brat real quiet. She just twist her mouth to the side. And I knows she still worried about what done happened wit that Betty Jean. So I whisper to'er. "If she done told, she done told. Ain't nothing we can do about it."

Farther down the road when we come to Miz Maylene's house, she setting on the front porch with a paper sack. Eating that Georgia clay.

Time she sees us coming she hollers at us. And we hollers back. "Hey there Miz Maylene. How ya been doing?"

Miz Maylene push back in her rocking chair and raise the tail of her dress up 'cross her knees. "Just fair to middling," she says to us. Then I sees why she been feeling poorly. She got her stockings rolled down under her knees. And they twisted in a big ole knot on the side. I hope she be knowing if you don't stop having them knots real tight they can cut off your circulation. And yo' blood'll be backing up. And backing up. And pretty soon all her blood'll be piled up so bad her eyeballs gon' be bulging right outa her head. And she ain't gonna be able to see daylight or nothing.

But I don't tell'er that 'cause I don't wanna make her scared. So I just act like I ain't paid it no attention. Miz Maylene just about old as Moriah, so she liable to go into some kind of calniption if she knowed what shape she in. Just start trembling and bucking and pass right out, here on this front porch right in fronta my face.

So I just says, "Miz Maylene, don't worry none. Yo' stockings might not be too tight." Miz Maylene looks at me like I done gone foolish in my head. Then she let out a grunt and go back to eating that dried-out clay. She try to offer us some. But we say no thank ya and go to talking about something else.

"Where Mr. Homer at?" Maybaby look 'cross the yard. "He ain't sick or nothing, is he?"

"Naw, he still gitting around." Miz Maylene reach in her paper sack and bring out a big hunka clay. "Ain't him that's ailing. Ralph Daniels' hogs is. That's where he at now. On the back tending to'em."

"Well Miz Maylene," Maybaby tells'er, "we best go on to the house so's we can take these bundles off Gertude's back and put'er in the shade outa this hot sun."

"Why don'tcha git on down to Moriah's Pond. Stick yo' foots in. Cool 'em off some."

"Naw, can't be doing that, Miz Maylene," Maybaby tells her. "Moriah says she gotta draw the line. Put a limit on going in the water till all our work did."

"Well, y'all younguns best hop to it."

Maybaby don't say nothing. She just turn Gertude around and we hurry up and walk past Miz Havana's, down to Moriah's. Maybaby the only one still got chores and not allowed in the pond. Me and Brat don't take no time to go neither. We piping hot and wanna cool ourselfs off real fast. So we just step in the tin tub 'long wit Maybaby and splash rain water all over our legs. When we done we don't wipe 'em off either. We just let 'em air-dry. Just go on round on the front where Uncle Curry setting at and let 'em dry on they own. Uncle Curry he nodding. Setting with his chair tipped back, leaning against the house.

"Uncle Curry, you 'wake?"

"Wake . . . Course I 'wake." Uncle Curry's head jerk up. "Just resting my eyes a tad. Every shut eye ain't sleep, gal. Dog bite 'it."

But I knowed Uncle Curry was half 'sleep 'cause his head was bobbing. But I don't dispute his word or nothing. I just take me a seat next to Maybaby and them. Setting on the porch where the hickory nut spread a lotta tree shade. Me, Maybaby, and Brat. All in a row. Swinging our legs. After a while Uncle Curry look over where we at and plucks him a straw from the stick broom.

Then he gaze off in space. Like he thinking on something real hard. Then he look back at us.

"This here a mighty strange world us living in."

"Whatcha mean, Uncle Curry?" Maybaby wants to know.

"Now take them cats . . ." Uncle Curry breaks off a piece of straw and pick his teeth. "Some got four legs and some walks on two."

"Two?" Now Brat twist all the way around. "I ain't never seen one of them before."

"Me neither," I says right quick.

"Ain't never?" Uncle Curry set his chair up straight. Flat on the floor. Looking dead at us. He don't crack a smile or nothing.

"Mean to say y'all ain't never heard of no two-legged cat?"

All us shake our head.

"Naw sir."

"Then I'd say y'all got a lotta learning to catch up wit." Uncle Curry lean back in his chair and look off 'cross the road.

"There some walking amongst us this very day. Yes sir. Sometime they can be a member of yo' own household."

"For real, Uncle Curry?" Now my eyes stretching so big I think they gon' pop right out. "How you know 'em? "

"Mind ya now. If you run up on one, you'd know'em right off."

"How—how they look, Uncle Curry?" Brat's eyes all

big too. "They look scary?"

"Dog bite'it." Uncle Curry sneak in a grin. "Think they look just like y'all. Setting there wit them ashy legs. Better go grease 'em."

"Ah-h-h Uncle Curry," I says, sticking my legs out. Looking at'em all scaly and white. "You just fooling us, ain'tcha Uncle Curry? Ain'tcha?"

Uncle Curry lean back. Propping his chair up against the house. Grinning. "Yes sir. Y'all ain't nothing but plain ole ash cats."

Now I knows Uncle Curry funning. Just playing wit us. So I hop off the porch and start dancing around popping my fingers.

"Ash cat, ash cat,
Where ya been?
Round the house
And going agin."

Maybaby and Brat jump down and do just like me. Popping their fingers and everything. And we keep on. All the way in the house. Then we find some Royal Crown hair grease and rub some on our legs so we won't be looking like no ash cats. Then we hears Moriah holler at Miz Maylene. So we stop what we doing and takes off down the road, to meet up with her.

"Moriah, what you done brung us this time?" I says, eyeing the bowl where I knows our supper at.

"Oh a little bitta this. A little bitta that," she says

looking down at me.

"Then I'm gonna tote it for you." I ease the dish outa her hand and take it on in the house.

I look down at the table. At Moriah's hand spooning up black-eyed peas and rice. I keep waiting for her to bring up about Betty Jean. And I know Brat waiting too. 'Cause she just picking at her food. Ain't hardly touched a bite. So Moriah wanna know what's wrong. And Brat just say, "Nothing." But I knows what the matter is. She worried, same as me. But Moriah don't mention one word about it. She just question Maybaby about sprinkling Miz Riggs' clothes so's she can iron'em. Then she set down in her chair.

"Lordy, these poor feet of mine feel just like fire."

Moriah stretch her legs out and lean back. Then I hears Uncle Curry coming wit his walking stick.

"Curry," she says to him, "you feel like eating a little something?"

"Had me a li'l something a while back," he tells'er, and go on where his room at.

"I want some more if Uncle Curry not gon' eat none," I says to'er.

"Annie Rye, you ain't had a nuff yet?" Maybaby says. "Gonna take all that food, then can't eat it. Yo' eyes just bigger than yo' stomach."

I lays my spoon down. Then I roll my eyes right at Maybaby. I feels like saying, "Ah-h-h shut up, Maybaby. Ain't nobody's eyes bigger than yourn. Witcha pop-eyed self." But I don't. I just keep my feelings to myself.

'Cause Mama'll be all over us just like bees in a hive. If she knowed we was at Moriah's cutting up. Showing off and going on. Not to mention what Betty Jean probably done said. So I gotta find a way to butter Moriah up. Stay on her good side. So's I can slip outa some of this trouble.

"Moriah," I says, easing up to her chair, "want me to pour some water on yo' feet so's they'll cool off some?"

"Baby, that sound real good. Go on over there and bring Granny the wash pan."

"Here ya go, Moriah," I says, sliding the wash pan under her feet.

Moriah leaning back in her chair while I pour water over her feet, and I'm trying to figure out why she ain't mentioning nothing about what went on today at Mr. Daniels'. The best I can figure, it done slipped her mind and she probably gonna lower the boom later. Or else her memory gone weak and she don't remember nothing a'tall. Then I hears her say, "By the way, Betty Jean told me about what happened today."

Me and Brat eyes meet. We in deep trouble.

Moriah set up in her chair. I sees her out the corner of my eye. Looking at me.

"Y' all wanna tell me what went on? Betty Jean sho nuff gave me a earful."

I draw up all stiff. Looking down at the floor. Listening at Brat talk nervous.

"S-s-she did?"

Moriah lean back. "That child told me everything. And then some. I declare. Almost worried me to death. Telling me how y'all showed her all this good stuff."

"She did?" me and Brat say at the same time. Like we hard of hearing or something. Now Moriah wanna know what else we done.

"Nothing, we just showed her some of our tricks," I tells'er.

"Well," Moriah says, "musta been some kinda tricks. 'Cause Betty Jean couldn't talk about y'all a nuff."

Now me and Brat looking at each other smiling. Then I start thinking. Why Betty Jean doing this? Why she ain't laid the blame on me and Brat 'bout her falling out that swing? She ain't normal. No sir. She sho ain't. And I try to make some sense outa that Betty Jean, after I lay down. Trying to figure why she act like she do. But time I close my eyes good, it's yesterday already.

Chapter 3

Washday

I didn't even hear the rooster crow. But I hears Moriah stirring around. And I knows morning done come. So I go on and git up.

When I opens the back door, everything up by the house all gray. And way back off in the woods all dark. I can't even make the trees out. The night still caught in'em. Now I hears that ole rooster crowing. Cock-a-doo-dle-do-o-o. And I know this here Wednesday. Moriah's washday.

I go drooping down the back steps. Then I hear Maybaby and Brat come down behind me.

"Annie Rye." Maybaby tapping me on the shoulder, sleep still in her voice. "I'll pump the water if y'all tote it."

"M-m-m-huh," I says, taking me a long yawn.

"Then take some of them buckets and come on." Maybaby already crossing the back yard. "Y'all hurry up. We ain't got all day."

I stand there gazing at the buckets, my eyes half shut. "Don't be rushing me first thing in the morning. My bones ain't woke up yet."

I look around for Brat. But she already got her buckets and heading towards the pump.

Shucks. Ain't no use rushing over to the pump. It'll still be setting in the same spot when I git there. I take down two buckets where they hanging at over the wash bench. Then I drag off past Miz Havana's chicken coop, where the pump setting out back betwixt her house and Miz Maylene's.

I set my buckets down so's Maybaby can pump them full. Then I tote 'em all the way back 'cross Miz Havana's backyard and dump water in the big black pot Moriah use for boiling her clothes in. Me and Brat traipse back and forth lugging water till the iron pot over half full.

Then after Maybaby done starting a fire under the pot all us go on back in the house, where Moriah whipping up some of them flapjacks. And they be smelling all over the house.

"Moriah," I says to her, "how long 'fore we eat? My belly growling."

"Soon as y'all set down." Moriah tighten her apron strings and turn around. "Fire going under the wash pot?"

All us nod yes'm, and Moriah set a heaping platter of flapjacks down on the table. And sugar syrup along wit'em. Soon as me and Brat all stuffed, me and her go on out the door and start filling the rinse tubs.

By now a little slither of sun inching over the trees, and Moriah scrub clothes on the scrubboard. She scrub Uncle Curry's, too. Rubbing'em real good with a hunka that lye soap she done made outa some lye, ole rank grease, and cracklin' skins. Time the water scorching hot, Moriah mash them clothes down in the pot where she done dropped some of that lye soap. Soon as she do, them clothes bubbling up. And she mush'em down again with a old ax handle. A battlin' stick, she calls it.

And when them clothes done boiled a good fashion, Moriah hold'em up on that washing stick and lets the hot water drain back in the pot. Then we rinse 'em two times from tub to tub. And when we hangs'em on the line, they white as white. Uncle Curry's shirts, too. Sheets and all. Not a dingy spot on em. And when I hoist the prop under the clothesline, the tail of them sheets just flapping and snapping. Cracking like a whip. And I can smell that good ole scent. Lye soap mangled up in the air. Stirring in the breeze. I feels just like running up to the line and hugging the sheets. Burying my face deep in'em. Wrapping myself up in the washday smell.

Then outa clear blue sky Brat saying to me, "Betty Jean nice, ain't she Annie Rye?"

I frowns my face up. "What Betty Jean got to do wit anything?" I says to'er.

Brat hunch her shoulders up.

"Why you thinking about Betty Jean anyhow?" I say.

Brat push her shoulders up again. "I don't know. I was just thinking 'bout how she act towards us. How she offer us stuff all the time. And she ain't tried to put the fault on us for falling out the swing."

"M-m-m-huh. I been doing me some thinking too," I

tells her. "And I got that girl pegged just right. I knows why she didn't tell. Probably 'cause she wanna have something hanging over our heads. So's she can hold it against us. So's she can git us in some trouble."

"Nope," Brat says, shaking her head. "You got it all wrong, Annie Rye. She done proved it."

I look off in space. "Ain't proved nothing to me."

"That's 'cause you don't wanna give'er a chance. She don't tell everything she know."

"How you know that?"

"I know," Brat says, whispering in my ear, " 'cause I felt Betty Jean hair one time. And it feels just like corn silk."

"Brat!" I wheels around. "You been had yo' hands in that white girl's hair? You know you ain't s'pose to do that," I tells'er, shaking my finger. "You gon' git it if you git caught."

"Naw I ain't. 'Cause Betty Jean don't care. She let me."

I sees it ain't no use trying to tell Brat nothing. So I go back to doing what I was doing. Sucking up that good ole washday smell. And I'm still taking me some more sniffs when Maybaby go to calling me from the house. I don't even turn around. I just keep doing what I been doing.

"Annie Rye. I know you hear me. So quit acting like you don't . . . Moriah say come on in here, so's we can heat some warm water.

"Why?" I says back to'er. My face tooted up. Sniffing.

" 'Cause we gotta wash our heads so's Miz Maylene

can do'em."

A little while later, all us washing our hair over the tin tubs setting by the back door. When we all done we plaits it in half-done plaits. Sticking out every which way. Then gon' round the back way to Miz Maylene's after it done dried.

"Miz Mayle-e-n-e," Maybaby calls, knocking at the door. "It's me. Maybaby."

"Come on," we hears her say. So me and Brat gon' in. Right 'long wit Maybaby. Miz Maylene setting at the kitchen table eating that Georgia clay. Just like I knowed she would.

"Y'all have some," she says, holding the paper sack up.

"No thank ya, Miz Maylene," we says to'er.

"Well, you welcome to it. Got some more in there under the dresser. And there plenty more where that come from." Miz Maylene push back in her chair and raise the hem of her dress 'cross her knees like she always do. "Which'cha y'all first?"

Brat she step right up and takes her a seat next to the wood-burning stove where Miz Maylene got her straightening comb heating at.

"This here hair twigged up mighty tight," Miz Maylene says, loosening Brat's first plait, "hope it be dry." Miz Maylene comb through Brat's hair she just got loose. And it spring right back. All bushy and kinked up. Brat she squinching up and frowning. And I knows why. 'Cause it be hurting like somebody pulling yo' brains out.

38

And time Miz Maylene bring the hot comb down to Brat's head, Brat just ducking and dodging. Dipping her head first one way then the other. Miz Maylene lay the straightening comb back on the stove.

"Now either we gon' do this hair. Or either we ain't. Which it gonna be?"

"I want it did." Brat whining.

"Well then—hold this head still. And when I git round to where your ear at, hold it down wit your knuckles flat so's I won't knick ya wit this hot comb."

Miz Maylene pick up the hot straightening comb by the handle and pulls them iron teeth through the plait she already combed out. Blowing all while she pulling. But it don't do no good. Brat hair sizzling and frying. Just like bacon. And Brat she all frowned up. And I knows it feels like her scalp hotter than a wood-burning stove. But when Brat all done I go on and be next. Gon' and git my brains burnt. But I knows I gon' be real good-looking when Miz Maylene done got my hair all straighten. And sho nuff. I peeks in the looking glass. Primping. Smoothing it back. My hair all slick to my scalp. Not a kink nowhere in sight. Even my kitchens—my hair round the edge of my neck. They laying flat too. All slick to my scalp. So I go to smiling at myself. Grinning in the looking glass. Hot-toe-mighty knows. I be sharp.

By the time Miz Maylene done wit Maybaby's hair, Moriah through fixing supper. Then after all us done had our fill, we just set around on the front porch doing nothing. Me, Moriah, and Maybaby and them. And Uncle

Curry just up and say how he got him a hankering for some blackberry dobee. And how some sho would taste good right 'long in now.

I knowed what Uncle Curry was gitting at. So I cut my eyes at Maybaby and she hunch Brat. We all done caught on. Uncle Curry hinting around for us to go pick him some of them blackberries. 'Cause he wanna fix hisself a dobee.

So Maybaby she says to him, "Uncle Curry, we'll go pick you some. Won't we, y'all?"

"Sho nuff?" Uncle Curry ask like he ain't knowed what was going on.

"Yeah, Uncle Curry, we'll go pick ya some," I tells him. I knows Uncle Curry can't go pick hisself none on account of his leg and all. And his having to git around on a walking stick.

On the way down the road where the blackberries grow at, we see Mr. Homer running wild, waving his spider arms in the air. Must be Mr. Ralph Daniels' hogs done bust out again. Yep. They did all right. Now we see'em. Scattering all over the place. Me and my sisters would've lent him a hand hemming'em up but we hafta pick Uncle Curry his blackberries and go on back to the house before nightfall. So we hurry on down to the patch so's we can git done.

All while we picking, my mind on them hogs. Trying to figure out if they might've run off in the pond. 'Cause that might not be too good. Them being sick and all. 'Cause if they trample up the pond while they ailing, we might not be able to go in no more this week. Maybe next week neither.

But Maybaby don't seem to be worried none. She say probably them hogs miles away from there by now. 'Cause they wasn't even running that way. She say them hogs not even thinking about going in that pond. Maybaby try to act like she knows just what them hogs gon' do. Maybe Maybaby right. Maybe they won't run in the pond and put the heebie-jeebies in it, maybe them hogs wasn't even thinking about it.

But when we make it back to the house we finds out them hogs was thinking about it all the time. And they muddied up the pond a good fashion. Not only that. Moriah tells us them hogs had greasy salve rubbed on'em where Mr. Homer was trying to cure'em. And now they got it in the pond, too. So none of us can go in till Mr. Homer and them take some croaker sacks and skim the greasy film off the water. So I wanna know when that gon' be. And Moriah just says after it done rained.

"After it done rained!" we all say at the same time. Now my face gits all frowned up.

"But Moriah, there ain't been a dark cloud in the sky. It might not never rain."

"Li'l Rye. Take them wrinkles outa yo' face. Gon' be looking old 'fore yo' time."

I unfrown my face and looks down at the floor.

"Now," she says to all us, "what happens will happen." Moriah's finger start pointing towards the ceiling. "The Good Master bring things about in his own good time.

Now y'all go on and make yo'self useful."

Shoot. Can't trust nobody these days. 'Specially no hogs. I brush the broom hard against the porch. But before I barely sweep one board, Moriah saying for me not to be sweeping the porch off since the sun done already gone down. 'Cause I might be sweeping somebody outa my family. And she not in no mood for a burying. So I lay the stick broom up 'side the wall, trying to figure how to keep from going up to Mr. Ralph Daniels' in the hot sun. Worst than that. Miz Nicey-Nice gon' be all up in my face.

So I do my bestest thinking. Got my thinking cap on and everything. But I can't think up nothing. And if I didn't need nothing to eat I wouldn't even go. Sho nuff wouldn't. I'd stay right here in the cool shade setting with Uncle Curry. Have me a straight chair just like him. Propped up against the house.

Chapter 4

Dead Wrong

The house still holding that good ole sweetness when morning come, from when Uncle Curry fixed his dobee last night. We don't beg for none or nothing. 'Cause he already done give us a taste. Now we ride on up to Mr. Ralph Daniels' place where Moriah at, so's she can fix us something to eat. And we can bring back the wash on Gertude.

Soon as we done ate, me and Brat go set on a bench outside the kitchen waiting for Maybaby to bundle the wash. And up walks Miz Nicey-Nice with a soda water. Sipping on it like she always do. Looking at me and Brat, just grinning. She got them big ole bow ribbons in her hair too. She pulls on one and takes her another swallow of that R. C. I sees Brat looking at that soda water like she want some. Just begging with her eyes. My eyes on Betty Jean too. Not 'cause of her soda water or nothing. I just wanna see how long 'fore she bragging how she kept me and Brat from a good skinning. How she done saved our hides and all. Just waiting on her to say it. Tell us straight out how she can make things real bad for us if she had a

mind to. Then she'll be strutting in our face acting all high
and mighty. So I just wait on her to go on do it. But Betty
Jean don't. All I hears her say is, "Y'all been at Moriah's
Pond lately?" And 'fore I can answer back, before I
can say none of your B-I-Z, Brat she saying, "We been
fishing some," gitting all happy wit Betty Jean. Brat know
full well she ain't been doing no fishing. Just had her pole
sticking up in the air. And anyway, I don't know why she
and Betty Jean trying to act like we bosom buddies.
'Cause we ain't. We sho ain't. Betty Jean just running her
mouth so she can have something to say. Just like she
doing now.

"Maybe I'll go wading wit y'all sometime," she says,
sipping on that soda water. Brat she git all glad. Grinning
all over herself. Betty Jean she do too. Not me. I just
stretch my lips real quick and let'em go back in place.
'Cause I knowed Betty Jean was telling a big fat story.
She won't be coming nowhere wit us. Not if Mr. Ralph
Daniels had anything to say about. She being his kin and
all. And me and Brat being colored like we was. Mr.
Ralph didn't take kindly to that sorta thing. Colored and
whites mingling. Taking up time with each other. Playing
and going on. Betty Jean she knowed too. But she still
always up under me and Brat. Always up in our face.
Offering us stuff. Just listen at'er.

"Y'all want some soda water?" she says, holding the
bottle out to me and Brat.

I shakes my head. I ain't gon' be catching the
heebie-jeebies from nobody. Not me. All them dregs just

floating around in that bottle. I sho don't want none. Brat do. She takes her a big swallow out that white girl's soda water. And before she can pass it back to Betty Jean, Mr. Ralph Daniels walks up. Brat hands it back real quick. But Mr. Ralph hawknose Daniels done already seen. He gives me and Brat the real mean eye. His hog jaws blood red.

"What's the meaning of this?" he holler at us.

Brat draw up all stiff. Stuttering. Scared and can't git her words out. So I tries to tell him it ain't our fault. But he won't listen. He snatch me and Brat by the arm and pull us in the kitchen where Moriah's at.

"Moriah, Brat here been drinking outa Betty's bottle. Now Moriah, you know we can't be allowing that." Mr. Ralph let me and Brat loose and push us up to Moriah. "You chastise this youngun . . . you whip'er or I will."

Then he takes his strap off and hands it to Moriah. I can tell Moriah don't wanna do it. 'Cause she got a hurt look on her face. So I beg'er "Don't" real hard, water in my eyes. Moriah never say nothing. She still hold on to the strap. So I tries to tell her, "She give it to'er, Moriah. Betty Jean she give it to'er." Moriah tells me "Hush." And she go ahead and whip Brat anyway. Right there in front of Betty Jean, God, and everybody.

When Moriah let Brat loose she run out on the back porch. Crying. Then Moriah gives us a good talking-to and make us take Gertude on back to the house.

On the way I don't say nothing. Maybaby she quiet too. I know she don't like it neither. Brat gitting a whipping on account of that white girl. O-o-o-o-u-we-e-e.

I feels like stomping that Betty Jean.

I look over at Brat, and she walking looking down at the ground. Water running out her eyes. So I go over and pat her on the shoulder. "If they never wanted you to have that ole soda water she never shoulda offered." Water still coming down Brat's face. "Don't cry, Brat. When I grow up I'm . . . I'm gon' buy you some soda waters. A whole heap of'em. All by myself."

Brat look up at me sniffling and rub more tears outa her eyes. "You will?"

"Yep. A whole carload of'em." I squeeze her up real tight. And we catch Gertude's rope, helping Maybaby take Moriah's ole brown mule back to the house.

I didn't like Mr. Ralph Daniels much after that. Causing Brat to have that whipping. And Betty Jean she know she offered that soda water to Brat. Brat didn't just reach up and snatch it or nothing. And Betty Jean didn't say nothing. Not a mumbling word. She better not never come running up in my face again. Never. Wit her ole chicken-neck self. She not no better than her granddaddy is. And Mr. Ralph not too much to speak of. Not after what he done. It was wrong. Dead wrong. And time Moriah come home, I tell her so.

"Moriah, it ain't right Brat having to git that whipping," I says all loud. Then I git quiet and roll my eyes down at the floor. "You . . . you shoulda never did like he said and whipped her anyhow."

Moriah takes a deep breath. "Li'l Rye, it's best to whip

yo' own—'stead of having somebody else lay a hand on'em."

"But how come she had to have a whipping in the first place? I tried to tell you it wasn't our fault. But you wouldn't listen."

"I did what I had to do. What was best for all of us. If I hadn't whipped Brat, Mr. Ralph would've. And I couldn't have done a thing about it. And it woulda hurt me to my heart to see that happen, so I done the next best thing. I whipped her myself."

I flop down on a stool next to Moriah. "But why? Why he act like that?"

"He set in his ways. Done come by it honest," she says, like it was nothing out of the ordinary. Like there was nothing strange about it a'tall. "That's the way his daddy was and his daddy before him. So it just done growed up in him."

"It's 'cause we Negroes. 'Cause we colored. Ain't it?" My eyes fill up with water. "That's why white folk treat us like they do."

Moriah got knowing in her eyes. Like she done been through this a whole heap of times. And then she just pats my knee and says things gon' be better by and by.

"By and by." What that s'pose to mean? I twist myself round on the stool and mumbles under my breath.

"I thought slavery time was over." I figured Moriah didn't hear. But she did.

"More than one kind of bondage, child. Now you go on and make yo'self useful. And I got to be gitting up from here myself."

"Yes'm." I walk a piece and look back at Moriah. She just set there with a faraway look on her face. Then I sees her chest heaving up. And she go to mourning. And it sounds like a rumbling coming outa her. Like a hurt so far down she can't dig it out. And she rock herself. And rock herself, way over into the night. Mourning out them old-time songs—filling the whole house from one end to the next. And the mourning don't have nowhere to go. So it goes to rest in the walls. And let the quiet come creeping up. And all I hears is that quiet. And Uncle Curry's cane against the wood floor. Rapping. Just rapping.

Chapter 5

Moriah's Pond

Next day Moriah say we don't have to worry none about coming up to Mr. Ralph Daniels' house where she gon' be. 'Cause she done fixed us some hoecakes and gravy. I was sho nuff glad. 'Cause I don't feel like laying one eye on Mr. Ralph Daniels. And I don't care what Moriah or nobody say. Might don't make right. Not in my book it don't. And I won't be forgetting it neither. And I know Brat still feeling bad about it too. 'Cause she ain't said two words. Not since Moriah left the house. Now it's way up in the day. And she still off to herself. Just setting on the steps with her hands tucked in her lap. Looking pitful.

So I says to her, "Betcha anything if we go underneath the porch we could see us one of them ole doodlebugs. You wanna?"

Brat bow her head. So I know she wanna. So me and her crawl underneath the porch and hunt for a doodlebug house. Pretty soon we sees a teeny-weeny hole humped all around with sand. And we knows we done found us one. So we wiggle us a teen-ouncy straw from the stick broom down the hole where that doodlebug live at. And then we go to saying our saying:

> *"Doodlebug, doodlebug,*
> *Yo' house on fire.*
> *Doodlebug, doodlebug,*
> *Yo' house on fire."*

And that ole doodlebug come inching right out. Just like that. Brat looks at me, grinning. And I grins right back. Then before you could say scat, before that ole doodlebug figures he done been tricked, me and her was long gone. Racing down to the pond to see if Maybaby still got Gertude tied in the shade. She do. So I flop down against the tree where Maybaby all sprawled on the ground at. Brat she spread out too, belly down. Just like Maybaby.

"Me and Annie Rye we just seen us a doodlebug. And we coulda caught one too. If we'd wanted to. Couldn't we?"

"Too hot to go crawling round up under a house," Maybaby say.

"You sho nuff right, girl." Brat laugh. "Ain't a cool breeze stirring nowhere. And these gnats 'bout to drive me crazy. Just swarming round my face like they ain't got nothing else to do. Don't know why they wanna wallow in sweat. All they gotta do is light on the pond. There plenty water out there."

"Yeah. And y'all know what? Them bullfrogs and water bugs ain't sick or nothing. Ain't nothing happen to them," Maybaby says. "Maybe the water ain't all that bad. 'Cause the grease off them hogs ain't made 'em sick. They still gitting around like they used to. So I don't see why Moriah don't want us in the pond yet."

"Grease? I don't see no grease." I looks real hard at the water. If there was some grease out there, I'd be the first to see it. 'Cause I got good eyesight. Just like a hawk. So I tells'em, "No sir, not a specka grease nowhere."

Now me and Maybaby look at each other. And I can tell what Maybaby she thinking. Same as me, 'cause she got wishing in her eyes. So I says, "Maybe them hogs didn't mess it up bad like Moriah thought. Maybe they just muddied it a little bit."

"Could be Mr. Homer and them come down here and skimmed the grease off and ain't told nobody. 'Cause they wanted to surprise us," Maybaby put in. "And maybe it rained and we didn't know about it. And nobody didn't tell us."

"Yeah. That must be it," Brat says while we inching up to the water. Then she rubs her fingers together after she done stuck'em in. "You right, Annie Rye. Ain't no grease in it. It don't even feel greasy."

"Then it probably won't hurt nothing if we just wiggle our toes in," Maybaby says.

So I go ahead and dab my big toe in along wit Maybaby and them. Then all us step in. Both feet. And before you know it, all us splashing in that water a good fashion.

"Hey y'all," Brat hollers. "It feels real cool over here."

I start wading out towards Brat where the tree limb

dipping down like a crooked elbow, and Maybaby flops down right in front of me.

"Oops. I done slipped down in this water and got myself all wet." She laugh.

Brat do the same. I bust out laughing too. Then Maybaby says she gon' baptize me. And I tells her naw she ain't. 'Cause I ain't gon' be gitting my hair all wet for nobody. I just got it straightened with the hot comb. And I tells her so.

"Maybaby, I ain't gon' be going around wit my hair all packed down on my head like cockleburs. Looking like some little throwed-away child."

"You already look like one." Maybaby laugh and duck Brat under the water. Then Brat turn around and do the same to Maybaby.

When Maybaby and them come out the pond, they soaking wet. Head to toe.

"Girl, look at y'all. Y'all wringing wet," I says to'em.

"So?" Maybaby says. "Moriah ain't gon' know. Unless somebody go running they mouth." Maybaby's eyes fall right on me. So I looks off the other way.

"You gon' tell, Annie Rye?" Brat says, whining and going on.

"Yeah, she gon' tell, " Maybaby hollers out. "Run on, tattletale. Blab to Moriah."

Now Maybaby done got my blood to boiling. Done got me real mad. Calling me a tattletale. Saying I can't keep nothing to myself. I just looks at'er and roll my eyes.

"You gon' tell, Annie Rye?" Brat tap me on the

shoulder. And I knows she scared she in for another whipping. So I say I won 't tell.

Then her and Maybaby want me to promise and say right hand to God. So we all do. Promise we won't say a word. Not nary one. 'Cause if Moriah had any notion what done happened, about us going in the pond and all, she sho won't like it one bit. No sir. 'Specially since she done warned us beforehand. But Maybaby got a remedy for that, too.

"If Moriah wanna know why our heads all nappy I'll just say we got sand in it. So it had to be washed."

Real quick Brat tries to brush hers out. But it don't do no good. That sand mingled all down in her hair a good fashion. And I knows they in deep trouble. Maybaby knows it too. Now she want me to cross my heart.

So I says to'er, "Girl! What I done said. You want me to write it down in some blood? I don't hafta cross my heart. I done said I promise. Didn't I?"

Maybaby give me a hard look and untie Gertude. All the way back to the house Maybaby reminding us what we s'pose to do.

"Now y' all remember," she says to me and Brat, "I'll do most the talking. 'Cause I got it all mapped out. And if Moriah wanna know how we got dirt in our hair, I'll just say we was tussling and going on."

"We wouldn't hafta be scheming if you and Brat hadn't gone buck wild. Dunking in the water and going on. Splashing too much." I look down at my dress, wet almost to the waist. "Now y'all got me in trouble."

"Ain't nobody got you in nothing," Maybaby tells me. "You went on yo' own free will."

"Yeah, Annie Rye," Brat join in. "We didn't make you."

I stop dead in my tracks and twist my mouth to the side. "I know you didn't make me. My mama did. And if I was made again, I'd be homemade."

"Ain't no use trying to wiggle out, Annie Rye. You in just as deep as us."

"Yeah, Maybaby," I says, wobbling my head around, "but my hair ain't all kinked up. Ain't all knotty and wet. And all I hafta do is walk around outside a little while. And my clothes'll be dry just like that," I says, snapping my fingers. "Anyway, my underskirt easy to dry." I shows my slip and keep telling Maybaby like it is. "So if it was me by myself, I wouldn't hafta worry about nothing. Wouldn't hafta tell Moriah one thing. But naw. You and Brat had to go hog wild. Now you got me mixed up in this mess."

"Ah, Annie Rye, it ain't that bad," Maybaby decides. "All we gotta do is put some dry clothes on, and hang our wet ones out behind the fig tree. But first, somebody gotta sneak in the house and bring us some out." Now Maybaby looking right at me.

"I ain't going in there. Uncle Curry might see me."

"Ah, girl. Won't nobody see you. Uncle Curry nodding on the porch like he always do."

"Yeah, Annie Rye," Brat put in. "He probably half 'sleep."

54

"Well he coulda heard us down at the pond and woke up."

"Uncle Curry ain't heard nothing. And he won't hear nothing if you tip in the house." Maybaby still trying to push me up to go. "Anyway, Uncle Curry don't pay no mind to what's going on no way."

"How you know?"

" 'Cause I know."

"Well if you know so much why don'tcha go for yo'self?"

Now Maybaby all quiet. "I can't. I might track up the house." Maybaby squeeze more water outa her dress. "I'm too wet."

"Me too." Brat look down at the water draining down her legs. "Please, Annie Rye."

I look off in space. "Well, I reckon I will. This time," I tells'er. "But don't be asking me to do it no more."

"Naw we won't. Now go on. Hurry up. Maybaby shushing me.

"Don't be rushing me," I says, easing up the back steps.

Time I'm in the kitchen, I go sneaking and peeping. Looking round for Uncle Curry. Then I sees him through the front window. Setting with half his back propped by the opening. So I tiptoe over where the old trunk up against the wall. I raise the lid real slow. So it won't be creaking and going on. Then I peep around to see if Uncle Curry in the same place. He is. So I dig down in the trunk and find Maybaby and Brat some clothes. I dig down and pull me some out too. Then I go tipping 'cross the kitchen to the back door. Maybaby and Brat still looking like wet chickens. Clothes stuck right to'em.

"You got'em?" Brat says to me while I'm coming down the steps.

"Yep. I got'em," I tells'er, patting the bundle under my arm. "They right here."

"Let's take 'em round yonder. Behind the fig tree." Maybaby pointing way out back by the edge of the yard.

Soon as we outa sight, round behind the fig tree, all us change our wet things and spread'em out on some bushes. Then all us hightail it back to the house. Rushing before Moriah come home.

"Somebody in the kitchen," I whispers in between'em, while they scrub they heads over the tin tub.

"You just hearing things," Maybaby tells me.

"Naw I ain't. I heard something," I says, close to her ear.

"A-a-h-h, it's probably Uncle Curry."

Then we all look up and it ain't Uncle Curry a'tall. Moriah standing right in the door. Looking dead at us.

Chapter 6

Cupboards Store

"What on earth y'all doing washing heads? Say?" Moriah question us with her eyebrows all bunched up. So I knows we in deep trouble and I can't figure out nothing to tell'er. So Maybaby she speak up right quick.

"We was playing and got grit in it."

"Sho nuff did." Now Brat she jump in backing Maybaby up. "And it was mangled in there a good fashion. Wasn't it, y'all?" She says. Her eyes right on me.

I look down at the ground and don't say nothing. Then Maybaby jab me with her elbow. "It had sand in it all right," I tells'er.

Moriah take her a deep breath, and I know her eyebrows bunching up again. "Li'l Rye?" I hears her say.

My eyes ease up where hers at.

"Seems to me you had on something other than that 'fore I left this morning. Didn't ya?"

I swallow real hard. 'Cause tightness all in my throat. And I knows my words gon' git hung up in it. So I just says, "Uh-huh."

Moriah she still looking at me. Questioning with her

eyes. So I tells'er, "Yes'm. I did. But they got all messed up."

"You mean to tell me all y'all got'em messed up? Say?" Moriah's eyes go from me to Brat to Maybaby. But she don't give us no chance to answer her back. She just go on speaking her mind. "I may be gitting on in years. And the Lord knows some of these parts don't wanna work the way they used to. And I may seem a little feeble at times. But my memory ain't weak." Moriah prop her hands on her hips and rear back. "No'm. There ain't nothing a'tall wrong wit my thinking. And I know I made it clear as I could, y'all not suppose to go—"

I just knows Moriah gon' say "in the pond." I can tell it in her voice. I knows she figured out what we been up to. Maybaby she think it too. 'Cause she cut right in before Moriah done saying what she saying.

"But Moriah . . . ah . . . we . . . we didn't mean to git all . . ."

Moriah put her finger up for Maybaby to hush. Ma-n-n-n oh me. Now we all know we in big trouble. So we just hang our head. Waiting on Moriah to finish gitting her words out.

"Now, like I was saying," she goes on, "y'all not s'pose to go changing clothes anytime the spirit move ya."

My eyes buck wide open. Maybaby and them looking foolish too. Acting like they hearing done gone bad and they ain't heard what they heard. But Moriah said it all right. Said for us to keep the same thing on and stop changing so much. And didn't mention nothing about the pond. She just start back in the house and so I figures we safe. Home free. Then she turn back around.

"Y'all ain't off the hook yet," she warns. "And the next thing . . ."

Uh-oh. We ain't lucked out like I thought. Now she gon' lower the boom for real.

"Y'all a bit old to be wallowing in the dirt. 'Specially you, Maybaby," is all Moriah say.

I flops down on the wash bench. My knees weak as water.

Come Saturday, Maybaby and Brat's hair all kinked up. Seeing how Miz Maylene still a mite under the weather, and she ain't up to straightening it, they looking all bad about the head. So Moriah started to make 'em stay home and not come tagging behind her to Cupboards Store to git Uncle Curry his kerosene. But they went to begging. So Moriah let 'em come on. Now Maybaby and Brat walking behind us like some little throwed-away chilluns. I walks up front with Moriah. Skipping. Matching my steps to hers.

Pretty soon, after we done come way down the road, we meet up to one that crisscross the one we on. And yonder sets Cupboards Store right on the other side. It ain't hardly no bigger than a shoe box, not like the one they got in town. We don't go to that one none much. 'Cause it's a far piece to walk. So Moriah just mostly come to this one. And she done told us before we left the house to stand outside. So that's what we all do. Stand outside till Moriah come out with a humped-over white man to fill her can up. So's she can buy some kerosene for Uncle Curry, 'cause he don't have no 'lectricity in his room. He just got a kerosene lamp.

While Moriah doing that, I start gazing in the store window trying to see what I can see. And up pops—who else? Betty Jean. I wanna act like I don't see'er but she standing right smack dab in fronta my face. Saying hey and going on. And I'm just fixing to tell'er, "Move, girl. I can't see through you. Your daddy don't make no glass. You flesh and blood."

Then I sees Moriah out the corner of my eye, and she got hers penned dead on me. I look down in the dirt and rolls my eyes back up at Betty Jean. She got her nerve. Coming in my face. Strutting up to me like ain't nothing happened. I don't want nothing else to do wit'er. So I turns my head to the other side. And I hears her say again, "Hey, Annie Rye," all soft like.

"Hey." I mumbles down so low my lips ain't hardly parted. "Whatcha want, girl?"

"T-to . . . to say hey." Betty Jean fumbling over her words. "And—ah—maybe we can go doodlebug hunting like I done said before."

"M-m-m-huh," I says, looking off in space. I felt like saying "Liar, liar, pants on fire." But Moriah still got her eyes on me. So I just says, "I gotta go." Then Betty Jean reach out to catch my arm. Acting like there something she wanna say but don't know how. So I just pull my arm close to my side and tells her over again, "I gotta go."

Then I sees her over where Brat picking at her eye. Rubbing it and going on, standing beside Maybaby. Betty Jean trying to say something to'em. But they act like they don't wanna talk to'er neither. I know I don't. I sho had made up my mind to igg her. Pay her no attention at all. But Moriah had her eye on me all the time. 'Cause she knowed I don't think too much of Betty Jean after what happened. So on the way home Moriah gives me a good talking-to.

"Li'l Rye," she says to me while I'm walking beside her, "you just can't act any way you want. You could make matters worse. You hear what I'm saying?"

"Yes'm," I says to her.

"Long as I'm working for Betty Jean's granddaddy and living on his place, I'm beholding to him. And I don't want no confusion between you and Betty Jean."

I draws my mouth to the side. "It wasn't my fault. I didn't start nothing."

"I know," Moriah says, taking her a deep breath. "In these times we living in you don't have to. So it pays to hold yo' peace. You'll fare a whole lot better that way."

Moriah takes a long hard look down the road. "You don't have a full understanding just yet, child. Just keep living," she tells me. "Just keep living."

I reach and take Moriah's hand. I knows what she done meant. Mr. Ralph could throw her off his place if he had a mind to. And he didn't hafta have no reason to do it. Just 'cause he could. Just 'cause we was colored.

But shoot, I wasn't figuring on causing no trouble. I

just wanted Betty Jean to tend to her own business and leave me alone so's I can tend to mine.

Next time we see Betty Jean, me, Maybaby, and Brat, we leading Gertude home. And all a sudden here come this pickup truck just spinning up dust. Then I spot somebody hanging out the window. Betty Jean. And she just waving like crazy.

"Hey, Annie Rye, y'all," I hears her holler at us. Like we all buddy-buddy.

I don't wave back or nothing. I don't even open my mouth. Let her holler till her tongue drop out. I don't have nothing else to say to'er. Never. She can just keep waving from now on. She not going to be buddy-buddy with me. I screw my face up.

"Annie Rye, you see Betty Jean?" Brat says to me.

I looks off the other way. "I ain't noticed."

"That was her all right. I can tell 'cause she got them big ole bow ribbons in her head." Brat knuckle her eye while she talking.

"Why you keep on rubbing yo' eyes? You got dust in'em?" I look down the road where Betty Jean went. "That's just like Betty Jean and them," I says, "raising dust and causing trouble."

Brat look at me. Squinching and going on. "Naw, they was burning before then. Like they got fire in'em."

"Mine too." Now Maybaby rubbing hers. "I can't figure out what I got in'em."

"Maybe y'all got some of that hot pepper in'em at Mr. Ralph Daniels' this morning."

"Naw, I didn't have none. Did you, Brat?"

Brat shake her head, still knuckling her eye.

So I says, "I betcha it's from all this hot sun shining down in'em. It'll burn anybody's eyeballs out. So whatcha oughta do when ya git to the house is rinse 'em out wit some cool drinking water and let'em air-dry. Betcha anything. Come morning, they'll be good as new."

Chapter 7

Sore Eye

When I hears that rooster crowing I pulls the cover way over my head, and curl up real good. Now I feels somebody shaking on me.

"Annie Rye . . ." Brat sound like she still half 'sleep. "Annie Rye . . . Moriah say git up. She leaving now."

I rollover wit the cover tight under my chin. Shoot. Rooster crowing. Brat shaking my gizzards out. Might as well git up, I grumbles to myself. So I go staggering in the kitchen. Maybaby she still in her sleeping clothes too. In there slouching in a straight chair. Moriah standing where the light bulb hanging.

"Moriah . . ." I says, stretching my mouth in a big ole yawn. "Could . . . could I just stay at the house and not go up to Mr. Ralph Daniels'? I ain't hungry."

"Me neither." Brat come stand next to me. Picking at her eye all matted with yellow gook. Maybaby's eye that way too. Done turned all red like.

Moriah takes one look and figures it out. "Y'all got the sore eye. Maybaby, heat some warm water on the stove. Put a pinch of Epson salt in a basin and bathe them eyes.

And y'all make haste and come on up to Mr. Ralph's." Moriah talking and fixing her apron on the way to the door.

"Miz Riggs never got a chance to drop her ironing off here at the house. So make sho you bring Gertude. And make sho you don't come out bareheaded. Shade them eyes from the sun," she says, then pull the door shut.

That was a little over a week ago. Now they done got sore eye in the other eye, just like the first one. So Moriah she send around to other houses setting 'long the road, to see if somebody still got any rain water they done caught first part of May. So's she can wash Brat's and them eyes out wit it. But nobody got none. So after then Miz Maylene she drop by the house to see if there anything she can do.

"Lord a'mercy," is all she say, then start clucking the way hens do to them biddies. That's what Miz Maylene always do when she can't figure something out.

"Ain't never seen no sore eye like this," she tells Moriah.

Moriah's face got a puzzle look on it. Just like Miz Maylene's.

"Ya know, Maylene. It's beyond me. Them eyes due to be clearing up by now."

Uncle Curry he standing back listening at what's been going on. Watching Moriah and Miz Maylene.

"Dog bite'it." He tap his walking stick on the floor real hard. "Whyn'tya let them younguns go on out to the mule trough where Gertude been drinking at. And wash them eyes. Take away the soreness in no time."

Moriah don't swap words with Uncle Curry. She send Maybaby and Brat out on the back and wash they eyes in the mule trough. Just like Uncle Curry done said.

Old folks knowed a lot about healing and curing and things like that. Like if you got the chicken poxes or something like that. All you'd hafta do is go in the chicken coop and let them chickens fly over your head. Shoot. You'd be cured just like that. So I figures with Uncle Curry's know-how, Brat and them oughta be all healed up 'fore you can say dog bite'it.

But every day Maybaby's and Brat's eyes still looking bad. So Moriah hitch us a ride to town on Mr. Homer's wagon. She say nothing left but to git'em on in so's Doctor John can have a look at'em. Doctor John he the white doctor, so all us hafta go in the back door and set in the hall. Not in the front part like other folk do. When he come out he speak to Moriah and lead us to his doctoring room by a side door for colored people.

He check on Brat eyes first. Then Maybaby's. Looking straight in'em. And tell us Maybaby and Brat got some sorta infection that done set in. So Doctor John lay his eyeglasses down and start popping his tongue. Wanting to know if we been into something we ain't had no business.

We hunch our shoulders up, acting like we don't know nothing about nothing. I try not to look at Maybaby and start shuffling my foot on the floor. I can tell he know we ain't gon' be letting on about nothing even if we did know. So he don't question us no more. He just go on and tells Moriah about them drops. How Maybaby and Brat hafta put some in they eyes twice a day. But he never give her no eyedropper or nothing. So Moriah she just use a straw from the stick broom. And every single time she try to drop them drops in Brat's eyes, Brat start hollering and pulling back.

"Naw Moriah, wait . . . I . . . I ain't ready yet."

"What done got into you?" Moriah frowns at'er.

"You aiming for them eyes to be like this till kingdom come? Huh? That's what you aiming for? 'Cause if it is, you on the right track."

Brat bust out crying. "You . . . you gon' poke me in the eye wit that straw. I . . . I'm scared."

"Fix yo' face up now and come on over here." Moriah beckon for Brat. And Brat ease back up to the table. I can tell Moriah not pleased the way Brat been acting. I can tell 'cause one eyebrow hump up and the other one don't.

"Now child, you look," she tells'er. "Moriah got no time for you to be carrying on wit this foolishness. All being done is letting medicine roll off the straw in ya eye."

Brat hang her head, watching the floor. Still sniffling. "But . . . I . . . I could do it myself. You let Maybaby do her own."

Moriah give Brat a good hard look. Like she don't know if she can trust Brat's word. "Can I count on you to do like you say?" Moriah press her hands down on her knees and move from where she setting at. "You know we hafta git them eyes healed up.

Brat got her head still bent. Twisting her foot on the floor. "Yes'm. I'm gon' do it."

That been more than a week. Still Brat's eyes won't clear up none. Maybaby's did. And Moriah been asking Brat all along if she'd put that eye water in her eyes. And Brat kept saying yes'm. Now Moriah says it's awful strange how Maybaby's eyes well and Brat's still don't look too good. So Moriah pull Brat aside and make her tell the truth.

"Brat," I hears her say, "when was the last time you put medicine in your eyes?"

Brat hang her head down. "I dunno."

"Look up here," Moriah order her. "This got something to do wit that straw poking you in the eye. Don't it?"

Brat nod her head. So Moriah lay the law down to'er.

"From now on, I'll put the eyedrops in myself. Even if I hafta tie you hand and foot." And that's what Moriah almost hafta do. 'Cause every time Moriah fixing to put drops in, Brat start doing like before. Pulling back and going on. So Moriah grab her by the shoulders and shake her real hard.

I stay back in the corner. I ain't gitting in Moriah's way. No sir. I ain't never in all my born days seen Moriah worked up like she is. Her patience done run out. I know she ain't playing. One bit. And Brat she straighten up right quick.

Now that Moriah seeing after Brat's eyes, I figures they'd soon be cured. Good as new. After a while, sho as shooting, Brat's eyes look a hundred times better. Moriah say she don't wanna take no chances of'em flaring up again. So she say for Brat to keep out the sun. And she say for me to stay at the house and keep her company. And watch out for her. So me or Brat neither one hafta go traipsing off to Mr. Ralph Daniels'. We can set on the front porch with our backs propped up. Doing just like Uncle Curry do. And Maybaby take Gertude by herself and bring us something to eat.

I was glad too. Real glad. Not 'cause Brat had trouble wit the sore eye. Or nothing. I was just glad I could set in the cool shade. 'Cept when I hafta hoe Moriah's garden. And I be done wit that first thing in the morning. Clean them weeds out in no time flat. Then be back up on the front porch cooling my heels. Lazying around just like Brat.

I know Mr. Ralph he glad we ain't gon' be coming around too. He probably still think Betty Jean might catch something from somebody. Humph. I ain't particular 'bout being round her nohow. So that suits me. Yes sir. Suits me to a T. 'Cause I'm setting pretty. Like Uncle Curry always say, "got it made in the shade." And there a lotta tree shade spread over the front porch too. So me and Brat just lean back and fold our arms. Doing just like Uncle Curry.

All this time it seemed like Brat's eyes been healing just fine. Then one morning they start itching again. So I says to'er, "Brat, stop rubbing yo' eyes. Let me see how they doing."

Brat act like she don't wanna move her hands.

"Go on, girl. Move yo' hands out the way."

Brat draw her mouth to the side. Don't move her hands or nothing. So I pull'em down myself. When I do Brat got a monster face. Her eyes done swoll up big as cow eyes. Done swoll almost shut.

Maybaby still got her sleeping clothes on, so she tells me go fetch Moriah. And I strike out for Mr. Ralph Daniels' house. Gertude trotting all the way. At the back fence I tumble off before Gertude stop good. Hollering for Moriah. By the time I make it up the steps, Moriah she already out the back door. Mr. Ralph he right behind her. And I tries to catch my breath and talk at the same time.

"Moriah . . . you . . . you gotta come. Brat eyes they . . . they all. . ."

"All what?" Moriah grab me by the arm. "Say?"

"They all swoll agin, Moriah. Swoll real bad. Her face look like it too."

Moriah's apron dangling loose. But she don't take no time to fix it or nothing. She just light out towards home.

"Hold on," Mr. Ralph calls after her.

Moriah ain't listening at a word he saying. She don't even turn around or nothing. Mr. Ralph need not try and stop her. 'Cause Moriah steady stepping. Going straight down the road. She don't even look back.

"Moriah," he hollers again. "Wait up." Then Mr. Ralph swings around in his scrappy old truck and picks Moriah up.

"Make haste. Bring Gertude on to the house," she hollers back to me.

Time I climb on Gertude, here come Betty Jean. Following me out to the road.

"Brat real bad off, ain't she?"

I bob my head. And Betty Jean start picking at her fingers.

"I hope she feel better directly. And tell'er . . . tell'er I say hey."

I don't say nothing. I just look sideways at the ground. She ain't bit more studying about Brat—than Gertude is. And Gertude a mule.

"Make sho you tell'er now," I hear Betty Jean say. And I just flap my knees hard against Gertude. So's she'll gitty-up. So's I can make it back to the house.

Mr. Ralph done already sent a field hand for the doctor. Now he trying to act all nice and everything. But it don't change nothing. Don't make up for what he done. Sho nuff don't.

We set around the house the rest of the day, waiting for Doctor John. But he never make it till way over in the evening.

"Howdy, Aunt Rye." He nod at Moriah, pulling his hat off. And there a red rim left where his forehead sticking out. He don't say much else. So Moriah show him where Brat at. He take one look, then lean back in the straight chair, popping his tongue the way he done before. Then he let Moriah know right off that Brat's infection done flared up again. Something fierce. And it'll make a world of difference if he knowed what we been into.

"Y'all sho you ain't been bathing in no wash water that's been left in the tub from scrubbing clothes, didja?" He cut his eyes over at me and Maybaby.

And we tells him right quick, "Naw sir, we ain't been doing that." Brat say she ain't neither.

"Well, you done picked up something from somewhere, that's for certain."

Now Moriah got a funny look on her face. And my heart go to thumping like a wild bucking horse. 'Cause I know what she gon' say before she say it.

"Y'all be swimming in that pond where them hogs was at?"

"No'm," Maybaby says right quick. "We ain't been swimming in the pond since you told us not to."

Moriah don't say nothing. She just looks Maybaby straight up and down. Just like she got something in the back of her mind she not letting on. Then she follow Doctor John out on the porch where Uncle Curry setting at.

Soon as Moriah not in hearing distance, Maybaby sneak over where I'm at. Talking low and going on. "Ain't been swimming in the pond," she says, breathing on my ear, "we was playing baptizing. Dunking and going on. That ain't swimming. Is it, Annie Rye?" Maybaby nudge me in the side and I look down at the floor.

I guess Maybaby was right in a way. They never did no

swimming. Just dunking one another under the water. And more than likely this other medicine gon' cure Brat's eyes sho as gravy.

Next morning Brat wake up talking all crazy. Saying, "Where you at, Annie Rye?"

"Setting right here. 'Side the bed," I tells'er.

"Where? Turn the light on. So's I can see."

I stand up, looking at daylight coming in the window. "Stop teasing, girl. Ain't nobody playing."

"Annie Rye . . ." Brat reach out feeling for me. "Turn the light on."

I back up from the bed and bust out the front door. "Moriah! Moriah! Come quick!"

Moriah jump up, sending shell peas flying every which way. Uncle Curry he hobbling on his walking stick right behind her. The next thing I know, all us huddling round the bed.

"Brat, child," Moriah says to'er, "look at me."

"Where you at?" Brat sound like she fixing to cry. "Turn the light on."

"Don'tcha fret none, baby child," Uncle Curry tells'er. "We's gon' see after ya."

Moriah wave her hand in front of Brat's face. All Brat do is stare off in space with her eyes wide open. Asking Moriah, "Where you at?"

All us look from one to the other. Not saying what we know. Brat blind. And seems like none of us can find nothing to say 'cause we all choked up. All 'cept for

Moriah. She set down on the bed, rocking Brat. Telling her, "It gon' be all right. It gon' be all right."

Maybaby scared. I can tell. 'Cause she inch right up under me, shaking. And time Moriah go on the porch where Uncle Curry done gone, Maybaby say she wanna tell what happened. What went on down at the pond. But Brat go to wringing her hands and crying. She say she don't want another whipping.

I hug her up real tight. "Don't cry, Brat. I ain't gon' tell on you. I ain't gon' say nothing."

"You promise, Annie Rye. You promise." Brat squeeze my hand real hard.

"Ah-huh. I promise," I says to'er. "I ain't gon' say nothing."

Later on, when me and Maybaby round back by the fig tree, she start up again.

"Annie Rye, I'm scared about Brat. Maybe we oughta tell Moriah. Then Doctor John can think up something else to do. Her eyes done gone bad. She can't even see." I hear Maybaby sounding like she 'bout to cry. "What if she can't never see no more?"

I wheels around face-to-face with Maybaby. "You tell. I ain't. And when you do, Brat gon' be mad witcha. And she ain't gon' never trust you never no more. She ain't gon' even much speak to ya. Sisters s'pose to stick together."

"Don't be hollering at me, Annie Rye." Now Maybaby acting all huffy.

So I tells'er, "Don't be gitting all huffy wit me, girl. You so big and bad," I says, propping my hands on my

74

hips, "go tell. I dare ya. Go on. And you gon' be the champeen blabbermouth. And Brat gon' hate'cha. You s'pose to stick by what you say. No matter what. So I ain't telling."

"But we hafta."

"No, we don't." I looks Maybaby dead in the eye. "We don't hafta do nothing but stay black and die." I cock my head to the side. "Anyway, I done promised. Done give my word. And I ain't gon' be going breaking it. Not for you. Not for nobody."

Chapter 8

Wait and See

Brat ain't been able to see for two days now. And she got a high fever on toppa that. So I knows she done took a turn for the worse. Done got real low sick. Miz Maylene she come by and brung Brat some pot liquor. But Brat won't swallow none. She just curl up in a ball, groaning.

Shivers just start running all over me. And I can't be still. I keeps on rambling round the house. Moving from one spot to another. Acting like there something I aim to do. But ain't figured it out yet. Not Maybaby. She ain't moved a'tall. Just been setting 'side the bed looking at Brat. Uncle Curry he setting there too. Right next to Moriah. So then Moriah wanna know whyn't I find me a seat somewhere and rest my nerves. So I ease me a straight chair up in back of Uncle Curry. And try staying put.

Then I hears Moriah talking down low. Telling Uncle Curry how bad off Brat is and how she might never come around like she oughta. Now them little shivers squiggling all in my belly, so I fold over in my lap, squeezing it real tight. And I just feel like something else bad gon' happen. And I know my feelings ain't fooling me when Moriah lean over again. Talking in Uncle Curry's ear. And when I hears her say how she 'spects that sickness done moved up in Brat's head, done gone straight to her brains, I ball up in a corner.

Mercy. I never wanted Brat to be like she is. Ailing and all. And I sho nuff ain't wanted her to be dead in the grave. I scoot back farther in the corner, wiping my eyes. I knows she gon' hate me. Ain't gon' like me never no more if I go telling on her. But I gotta tell. I just gotta.

"Moriah," I says, inching up 'side the bed, "I knows how Brat and them got the sore eye like they did." I looks down at the floor. "They was dunking one another . . . baptizing . . . and . . . and got all wet-up in the pond."

"I was in it too." Maybaby come up next to me. "Ain't all Annie Rye's fault. We made her promise not to say nothing." Now Maybaby's voice got shaking in it. "She didn't want to."

Moriah press her hands on her knees and stand up. "And why y' all just thought to say something now? Why y'all didn't tell the truth before? Say?"

" 'Cause I done give my word. Done promised. 'Cause . . . 'cause I ain't wanted Brat to git another whipping. 'Cause she just had got one on account of Betty Jean. So I felt sorry for'er. That's why." Water start running out my eyes. "But I never wanted her to be like this. Honest. I just didn't want her to be in no more trouble."

Moriah set back down. "Li'l Rye, dry yo' face up. You

too, Maybaby. No sense beating yo'self over the head with this. What's done is done. And there ain't no going back and changing a thing."

Some water rise in Maybaby's eyes and slip down her face. "Yes'm. But . . . but . . ." Maybaby sniffling real hard. "S'pose she don't never . . . I shoulda knowed better, Moriah. I shoulda knowed."

"Now y'all listen to me," Moriah says, pulling us over 'side the dresser. "What y'all done wasn't bad. Wasn't good neither. Now it's a mighty fine thing to stand up for right. To keep yo' word and all. If keeping yo' word won't cause nobody hurt or harm. Won't cost somebody else they wellbeing." Moriah unpucker her apron and go on talking. "Now we gon' just put this whole matter behind us. Just be sho you git some learning from what went on. And put it in yo' mind to never let it happen agin." Moriah let out a deep sigh, fixing her apron.

"You don't need no punishment," she tells us. "This thing done beat you a nuff. Now y'all gon' back in there and stay wit Brat," Moriah says, shushing us away. "I'm gon' see if I can't send word by Homer for Doctor John. Now we know what we up against. Maybe there's something he can do."

Seems like it take the doctor forever to get to the house. When he do, he say he couldn't make no guarantee anything'll do any good or not. Even if she do pullout of this okay, wit the other medicine he done brung, he can't promise how her sight'll be. All we can do, he reminds us, is wait and see. So all us wait. Uncle

Curry he go from one end of the house to the other. Mumbling to hisself wit his cane rapping against the wood floor.

Since then me and Maybaby ain't doing much of nothing. Just moping wit our hands propped up to our jaws. So Moriah come stand between us.

"Where'd all these sour faces come from? Worry ain't never cured nothing," she says, hugging our backs. "Now y'all go on see after Gertude."

Me and Maybaby don't leave. We still leaning on Moriah.

"Go on now," she says, squeezing us like before. "See after Gertude."

Me and Maybaby drag on out the door. One behind the other. We don't much feel up to fooling wit no mule. But we go 'head and pump some water for Gertude's trough.

Then we hurry on back to the house. Before we hardly get in the door good, we hear Moriah laughing and talking to herself and figure something good done happened. And sho as shooting. It sho nuff did. Brat's fever done broke.

Now all Brat do is sleep. Come nightfall she ain't even opened her eyes or nothing and I wanna know if they gon' be okay. If Brat gon' be sick much longer. While Moriah fixing the covers on me, I says to'er, "Moriah," I says, "Brat gon' be able to see like she used to?"

"That's up to the good Lord. We just hafta be patient," she tells me.

Come sunrise me and Maybaby the first ones up. Even before Uncle Curry. And most the time his feet the first one to touch the floor. But me and Maybaby got the jump on him. Got us a head start. 'Cause we wanna see if Brat opened her eyes up yet.

"Call'er," I says, hunching Maybaby in the ribs while we standing 'side the bed.

"No, you call'er." She elbow me back, talking low same as me.

"Why . . . why y'all . . . why y'all mumbling and going on?" Brat sounding like her jaws all heavy and she can't hardly push her words out.

"Hey Brat," we says to her. Looking, trying to see her eyes.

"Hey-y-y," she says back to us. Her "hey" sounding far off like her first words done.

Me and Maybaby just nudging each other and going on. Trying to see who gon' say something next.

So I says, "Brat, you should see Maybaby now. Gir-r-r-l, ugly got the mug on her sho nuff," I tells her, just teasing.

Brat bat her eyes, squinching. "Y'all ain't clear. Y'all . . . y'all all foggy."

Now me and Maybaby grab hands. Just grinning.

"You must got yo' eyes right on Maybaby's brains," I says right quick, " 'cause they always foggy."

"M-m-m-huh, Annie Rye," Maybaby says, "you oughta know 'cause yourn is too."

Now me and Maybaby hunching each other and

80

laughing.

Moriah must've heard us making a racket 'cause she come over where we at.

"Good gracious. A lotta commotion going on in here. This child been sick a nuff without y'all damaging her hearing, too. Heard y'all clear out back."

"Brat done woke up," I tells'er.

"Woke up? Oh, y'all sho that wasn't the other way around?" Moriah got a smile in her voice.

"Uh . . . she . . . she still can't see like she oughta," Maybaby says right quick, trying to change the subject. "Everybody look all strange to'er." Maybaby start giggling. And Moriah frown at'er, putting her finger up so's she'll hush.

I knowed Maybaby's mind was on foggy brains. So when I look at her I feels a giggle starting to bust loose. Then I meet Moriah's eyes and clamp my hands over my mouth real fast.

"I declare. If y'all don't stop all this sniggling. You better. Ain't got no business tiring this child out. She need all her rest." Moriah lean over Brat. "Let me have a look at them eyes. M-m-m-huh. Swelling going down nicely."

"So pretty soon we'll know for sho how Brat sight'll turn out? Right, Moriah?" I says, tapping her on the arm.

Moriah straighten up and smooth her apron. "We'll know something one way or the other."

I didn't like the sound in Moriah's voice. Didn't like the way she said "the other."

"Ain't much we can do anyhow." Moriah sighs. "Just

hafta hope for the best."

Moriah oughta not said that. Hope for the best. Now I gotta use my champeen hoping. Gon' put the ole whammy on it. Hook my little fingers behind my back and say my saying way down low. Plus done spit on the ground two times in the same spot. Now I knowed Brat was gonna be almost good as new. Knowed it sho as gravy. And for real.

Later when I pass by where Brat laying at and she tells me go grease my lips 'cause they all dried up, I don't even git mad or nothing. I just be glad 'cause I knowed Brat's eyes working like brand new. And I don't look foggy to her no more. I go easing up where Moriah at, rocking on my heels. "Moriah. Guess what? I don't look foggy no more."

"Wouldn't be a bit surprised if ya had been." Moriah rolling dough out for her biscuits and she don't stop. "Got yo' head stuck in them clouds too much. Dreaming."

"Naw Moriah," I says, jerking on her apron string. "Listen . . ." I keep moving from one foot to the other. "Listen . . ."

"Li'l Rye, why you prancing round in the floor? You need a trip to the outhouse?" Moriah flatten her biscuit out. "I declare, child, if ya ain't looking foggy, you holding yo' water too long."

"No'm, Moriah. You don't git it, about Brat," I says, hopping round in the floor. "She can see. She can see clear as day!"

Moriah drop what she doing. Throw her hands in the

air, hooping and hollering. Just like a crazy woman. And Uncle Curry he got his walking stick rapping on the floor. Rapping real hard. Then all us—me, Moriah, and Maybaby—hooping and hollering. Shouting. Just like you do when you git yo'self baptized.

When all us collect our senses again, Brat propped up in Moriah's bed. And we figures she all right. 'Cause she setting up and everything. And her eyes seem like they good as new.

Then when we come up close, we know something still not right. Brat got white spots right on her eyeballs.

In a day or so, when Doctor John come, Moriah wanna know the whole story about Brat's eyes. Want him to tell her straight out how things stand. So he tells her straight out. Brat's eyes not bad as they been. And she'll be able to see okay. Then Doctor John he git sorta quiet, so I knows he fixing to tell us something we ain't wanted to hear. He clear his throat and tells us them scars won't never leave Brat's eyes. And she'd bear them from now on. For the rest of her days.

Chapter 9

The Grudge

Maybaby says we oughta thank our lucky stars 'cause it coulda been worse. Way worse. "Ain't had nothing a'tall to do wit no lucky stars," I tells her. "Was my champeen hoping what done it." Cause I knowed that's the way it worked. Just like I knowed somebody gonna come 'cause my nose been itching all day long. Even after Doctor John done been here and gone. My nose still itching.

So when I hear somebody knocking on the door I know it must be Miz Maylene. Coming by to see how Brat doing. 'Cause nobody much else come after sundown. But it ain't Miz Maylene a'tall. It's Betty Jean. Big as day. Standing there 'side her mama. My chest get all tight. All swoll up. Like it gon' bust.

"Is it Maylene?" Moriah wants to know.

"No'm. It's Miz Riggs, she done come for her ironing," I hollers back.

"Well child, don't just stand there taking up space. Let her in," Moriah tells me.

I move to one side. Miz Riggs she come in the house, saying how glad she is Brat up and about. Betty Jean she come in too. I don't know what for. Nobody don't wanna see her. I for one sho don't. And now Moriah tells me to offer her a seat while she fetch Miz Riggs' ironing. I look at Moriah and back at Betty Jean. Offer her a seat. Huh. She better set on her fist and rear back on her thumb. And I feels like telling her just that. But I go on and do like Moriah say.

"Betty Jean, you wanna set on this stool?"

She want to all right, 'cause before I got my words out good she done flopped down, looking at me, grinning. I don't crack a smile. Not nary one. Then I notice Betty Jean holding her hands behind her back. When she pulls'em out she got some soda water. Two big ole R.C.'s.

She hands one to Brat. Then to me. Brat take hers. I just says, "No thank you, Betty Jean. I don't feel like no soda water. You keep it."

Not Brat. She got her one. Her eyes all big. Just grinning. I don't see nothing to be grinning about. Not one thing. Coming round here wit that ole stinking soda water. I push my mouth out and move over by Moriah's bed. Betty Jean follow me.

"Annie Rye," she saying, "I feel awful bad about what done happened. 'Bout Brat having to git that whipping and all. I know I shoulda spoke up. Wasn't y'all's fault. Was mine."

I roll my eyes at the wall. And Betty Jean still go on running her mouth.

"I'm awful sorry 'bout the whole thing."

I don't even look at'er. I just keep looking off the other

way. I feels like saying, "Yeah, and sorry got drowned in a Coca-Cola bottle. Better swim in and drag him out." And ain't no sense of her trying to beg my pardon neither. Saying she sorry and wanting me to have that soda water. I don't trust that Betty Jean. Ain't believing a word she done said. Ain't believing her mama neither. I don't care what she telling Moriah.

"Like I mentioned before," Miz Riggs saying, "we all feel mighty bad about what went on. You know about that whipping Brat got and all. This Betty Jean's way of trying to make up for it." I hears Miz Riggs sigh real hard. "So Betty Jean took her own money and spent it on that soda water."

I twist my mouth to the side. Her money. If she wanna throw it away, go 'head. That's her B-I-Z. I still don't want none of her ole soda water. And her coming here don't prove nothing. Not one thing. Let her keep offering like she is.

"Here, Annie Rye. Take it." Betty Jean push the soda water at me. "I done brung it for you. Here."

Moriah nod her head for me to take it. I look down at my feet, then back at Betty Jean. Holding that soda water out for me to take it. But I don't.

"Li'l Rye."

I look up at Moriah. "Yes'm."

"I wanna speak to you. Excuse me, Miz Riggs," Moriah says to Betty Jean's mama. "Li'l Rye don't usually behave this way."

"You go right ahead, Moriah," Betty Jean's mama tells

her.

Moriah lead me back where the kitchen table at. Back by Uncle Curry's room.

"Li'l Rye, what's ailing you?"

I put my head down. "Nothing."

"So you mean to tell me you got this long face on account of nothing . . . say? . . . Li'l Rye, I'm talking to ya. Look up here."

"Who she think she is," I bust out, "coming in here wit her ole soda water after what she done. Huh. She can just keep it and drink it her ownself. 'Cause I don't want it. Not one drop."

I knows Moriah wanna say something else. But I don't stop, I keep on talking. "It ain't fair," I says, looking in Moriah's eyes. "It just ain't. People think they can git away wit treating you any kinda way and you s'pose to take it. Not me."

"Betty Jean knows she was wrong. She a goodhearted person. And she come to patch things up. To set'em right. To make up for what she did."

I git all frowned up and look off in space.

"That ain't no way to be, child," Moriah says, touching my shoulder.

I look back down at the floor.

"Well," she says, "I'm not gon' try and make you take the soda water Betty Jean done brought. That's up to you."

All this time Uncle Curry been setting in his room wit the curtain to his door open. So I go set next to him on the bed.

"Baby girl," he says to me like he calls us sometime. "I ever mention to ya 'bout that boxcar breaking loose that time?"

"Naw sir," I tells him, tracing stitches on the quilt. "You ain't told me nothing about it."

"Ain't toldja, huh? Dog bite'it." Uncle Curry rest his chin on his walking stick awhile. "Seems to me this come about 'fore yo' time. Way 'fore." Uncle Curry straighten up. "Well sir, as I recollect, a buncha fellas was fixing rails. Changing old track. And up whipped a thunderstorm. Come outa nowhere. Rain pouring like the bottom dropped outa a bucket. Them fellas struck out for the nearest shelter. A empty boxcar. Well sir, let me tell ya." Uncle Curry shake his head, popping his tongue. " 'Fore any of 'em had any notion what was going on— the boxcar broke loose from the resta the train. Headed down hill."

"Wit'em in it, Uncle Curry?" I says right quick. "Wit'em in it?"

"Yes'm. Wit'em in it. And the only chance any of'em had was to jump. All them fellas made it in one piece. 'Cepting for one. He jumped and that leg snapped like a twig. Sho nuff did. Yes sir. Nearly broke clean in two.

"Ooou-we-e-e, Uncle Curry," I says, squinching up, "that musta hurt."

"Yep, 'spect it did. Seeing how it was all twisted. And none of'em had no know-how 'bout tending to it. 'Cept for this one fella. Only thing about it—the one wit the busted leg wouldn't allow the fella to touch him. Refused his help. Hollering and saying all sorts of mean things against him. The fella overlooked what had been said. Willing to tend to the leg anyways. But the other one stuck to his guns. No how. No way. Naw sir. Was he gon' let that fella touch him." Uncle Curry git all quiet, looking off 'cross the room. And I shake his knee.

"Why, Uncle Curry? Why?"

"Well ya see, a long while back the fella that knowed how to patch up the busted leg had wronged him." Uncle Curry gaze off again. "Harsh words was passed between'em. And the thing was never settled. The one wronged nursed them hurt feelings. Held on to'em. Naw sir. Wouldn't put'em behind him." Uncle Curry let out a deep breath. "By the time the bossman got the doctor out to the camp my leg was real bad off."

"You mean that was you, Uncle Curry?" My eyes stretch wide open and I git all frowned up. "But . . . but why you act like that? Why you never let him help you or nothing? Maybe all he was doing was trying to make up for what he done. Just trying to beg your par—" I git all quiet, looking down at the floor. Uncle Curry don't say nothing, he just rest his head on his walking stick. And then I hear the front door creaking open, so I peep round the curtain. There's that soda water Betty Jean done brung setting on the stool. So I pick it up and take it to the front door where she at.

"Betty Jean," I says, "you done left this here soda water." And I hands it back.

Betty Jean looking all funny in the face. "You don't want it?"

I drop my head, watching the floor. Then I sees Betty Jean's feet moving towards the door.

"Betty Jean," I says right quick, looking up at'er, "It was mighty good of ya to bring me this here soda water," I tells her. "And I'd be right pleased to have it."

I could tell Betty Jean was glad now. 'Cause a big ole smile inch all the way 'cross her face. And then—'fore I knows it—one done inched all the way 'cross mines too.